Thunder Cave

Roland Smith

Hyperion Paperbacks for Children
New York

Acknowledgments

Stories are written in solitude, but they are never writ-
ten alone. I want to thank all of those who helped me
with this book, especially my wife, Marie, who helps
me in more ways than I'll ever know.

First Hyperion Paperback edition 1997
Text ©1995 by Roland Smith.

A hardcover edition of *Thunder Cave* is available from Hyperion Books for Children.

Printed in the United States of America.

13 15 16 14 12

Library of Congress Cataloging-in-Publication Data
Smith, Roland
Thunder Cave/Roland Smith—1st ed.
p.   cm.
Summary: Determined, after his mother's accidental death, to foil his stepfather's plans
for his future, fourteen-year-old Jacob travels alone to Africa in search of his father, a
biologist studying elephants in a remote area of Kenya.
ISBN 0-7868-0068-2 (trade)—ISBN 0-7868-1159-5 (pbk.)
[1. Survival—Fiction. 2. Fathers and sons—Fiction. 3. Masai (African people)—
Fiction. 4. Poachers—Kenya—Fiction. 5. Kenya—Fiction.] I. Title.
PZ7.S65766Th   1995
[Fic]—dc20
94-19714

The text for this book is set in 14-point Hiroshige Book.

PART I
New York

January 3
Kenya, Africa

Dear Jake,

The long rains are from March to May, and the short rains are from October to November. When these rains fail to appear everything suffers. Last year the short rains never came, and the watering holes have been hardened by the heat of the sun. If the long rains fail this year I don't know what will happen here.

A little rain changes everything—that's the remarkable thing about East Africa. A few days of rain can turn this hard grim land into a soft green landscape.

I'm setting up a new camp, and I don't have much time to write. I'll try to get another letter off to you in a few days when things settle down.

I hope you and Beth are doing well.

All my love,
Dad

Before . . .

All three of my parents are doctors, but not the kind that could make you well if you were sick. My mother and stepfather hold doctoral degrees in anthropology and teach at a university. My real father has a doctorate in animal behavior. He's a field biologist studying elephant behavior in Kenya. He says that Ph.D. stands for "Piled higher and Deeper" and that the only real advantage of having the initials attached to your name is the false respect you get when someone calls you Doctor So-and-so.

"Having a doctorate does not mean you know anything," my father has said. "In fact, in my experience it means almost the opposite. Some of the dumbest people I know are Ph.D.'s. . . ."

According to my stepfather, Sam, my father's "not wrapped too tight." Sam is always putting him down, which really ticks me off. I'm not sure what he's trying to accomplish when he talks like this. Afterward, he always says that he shouldn't have said anything. "It just makes me angry that he hasn't been there for you, Jacob. . . ."

And I usually don't say anything, because it's Sam who isn't there for me even though we live in the same apartment in New York City. I suspect that Sam is the kind of Ph.D. my father talks about. My father has *always* been there for me. Not physically, but he writes to me regularly and tells me what he is seeing in Kenya and, more importantly, what he is feeling. I used to show these letters to my mom but it upset her to read them, so I don't do that anymore, and I wouldn't think of showing them to Sam.

I haven't seen my father in a couple of years. Not since Mom married Sam.

"I imagine having a stepfather is not going to be easy, Jake. Not for you and not for him. I had a stepmother that I didn't get along with, and I regret it now, because she was really very nice. Take it easy on him. . . ."

Mom and Sam seem pretty happy together. They teach at the same university, have the same friends, and share the same interests. I do take it easy on Sam, because my mom is happy and there were a lot of years when she wasn't. When my father and she split up it was hard for both of them.

"Your mom and I love each other and we both love you, but we don't get along and we've decided that this is not the best environment to raise you in. . . ."

That was about four years ago, when I was ten. I remember the arguments they used to have—not the words, but the intensity. I would sit in my bedroom and listen to the shouts and the doors slamming. Through the window I'd watch as my father pulled his jacket around him and stomped down the sidewalk. He'd walk around the block several times and each time he got to our apartment he'd look up at our windows, then stomp off again. Sometimes this went on for a couple of hours and then finally he'd come inside. Afterward my parents would talk quietly. Every once in a while my mother laughed, and I knew that things would be all right.

But one day it wasn't.

When I got home from school they were both waiting for me. I could tell that my mother had been crying. My father said that he had quit his job as mammal curator at the zoo and that he was going to Kenya to study elephants, and he didn't know how long he would be there. He had funding for at least a couple of years, and if the research went well he would be funded indefinitely. There was no mention of our joining him in Africa, and in a few days he was gone. Soon after this the letters started coming.

I've learned a lot about my father from his letters, probably more than I would have if he had stayed. He never talked much when he was around me—not about himself anyway. He's Native American—a Hopi from Arizona. When my father was a kid, his father, Tawupu, moved the family to New York City so he could work on skyscrapers and then decided to stay. Taw, as we call my grandfather, loved New York—a love my father never shared.

I suspect that this was one of the main problems that my parents had. My father wanted to move back to Arizona. He often said that he felt that the city was eating his flesh. My mother usually laughed at this, saying that the feeling was "just one of those back-to-nature things." Apparently she was wrong.

They waited a couple of years before they divorced. During the separation my father came home a few times. After the divorce, even these brief visits stopped. But at least the letters kept coming.

One

After school I rode my mountain bike home in the rain. Before I went up to our apartment I checked the mail for a letter from my father. No luck—just bills and junk mail. I wheeled my bike into the elevator and punched the button for the fifth floor. I saw myself in the elevator mirror: an Italian-Hopi boy with rain-slicked black hair and brown eyes, a little on the thin side, like my father, but not altogether bad looking.

The doors slid open, and I walked my bike down the hallway and opened the door to our apartment. Sam and my mom wouldn't be home for a few hours. I dropped my helmet on the table and leaned my bike against the wall in the hallway. Sam hated this, especially when the bike was wet, but I don't know where he expected me to put it. The bike cost me five hundred dollars, and I wasn't about to leave it downstairs. I couldn't put it in my jammed bedroom. The only empty space in there was on top of my bed. I liked my bike, but not enough to sleep with it.

The light was flashing on the answering machine. I punched the play button on my way into the kitchen to rummage through the refrigerator.

Beep. "Hi Beth, this is Sally. Don't forget the meeting tomorrow night. Seven o'clock. I'll see you there. . . ."

There was some leftover lasagna from the night

before. My mom makes the best lasagna I've ever eaten. I took it out with the gallon of milk.

Beep. "Beth, Mary here. . . . Give me a call when you get a chance. . . ."

Lasagna is always better the second day. I put the last slab on a plate and put it into the microwave.

Beep. "Jacob? I guess you're not home yet. Ah . . . there's been a problem. . . . Your mother has had an accident. . . ."

I put the milk down.

"She was hit by a car while jogging. . . ."

I walked into the other room.

"We're at Providence Hospital. . . ."

I stared at the machine.

"Get a cab and come down here. Come to Emergency."

I played the message back. Hit by a car? She'll be all right, I thought. She has to be all right. I've got to get to the hospital. Then I thought, In evening traffic a cab will take forever. I wheeled my bike into the hallway. As I shut the apartment door I heard the microwave beep.

I wove my way through the snarl of cars and trucks. Horns blared, sirens sounded. The rain poured down on people shouting for cabs, covering themselves with umbrellas, hats, and newspapers. I cut in and out of traffic, ran red lights, skidding to a stop on the wet pavement only when I had to.

I raced into the hospital's emergency entrance and leaned my bike against the wall, not stopping to lock it. The automatic doors hissed open, and I was hit with a blast of heat and the smell of disinfectant.

The waiting area was filled with people. A man holding a wailing baby tried to bounce it into silence. An old woman sat quietly with a thick compress on her forehead with blood seeping into it. A man sat in a wheelchair, holding his arm, moaning. Another man, staring glassy eyed, clutched himself as he shivered. Sam was nowhere to be seen.

I got in the line in front of the information desk. I wanted to push past the three people waiting in front of me.

Nurses and interns with stethoscopes around their necks and clipboards hurried past. Was my mother's name on a clipboard? Was she all right?

"May I help you?"

"My mother's here."

"Your name?

"Jacob Lansa."

She checked her computer screen.

"I'm sorry, but we have no one named Lansa here."

"She has to be here!" I said. "I just got a call. . . ."

"I'm sorry, but—"

"Try Walters!" Sam's last name.

She typed the name and looked at the screen again.

"Oh yes," she said. "She's been moved to the ICU—the intensive care unit—on the third floor."

I ran to the elevator. On the third floor I gave my name to the nurse at the desk.

"She's in room six," the nurse said quietly. "Your father's in with her now."

My father's in Kenya! I wanted to shout.

"I'll take you there." She got up from behind the desk, and I followed her down the hall. The door was open, and Sam stood by the bed with his back to me, blocking my view of her. He turned when I walked in.

"Jacob . . ."

He looked awful. I walked over to the bed and saw my mom. Her skin was bluish gray. A tube came out of her mouth and ran to a pump that hissed rhythmically.

"She can't breathe?"

Sam shook his head. "Not on her own. Jacob, it doesn't look good."

More tubes were attached to veins in the back of her hand. One tube ran up to a bottle of clear liquid that bubbled as it dripped into her.

This isn't my mother! I kept thinking over and over again. *This isn't my mother. . . .*

"What do you mean it doesn't look good?"

"They say that she has a very poor prognosis."

"What does that mean?"

Sam turned away from me, hunched his shoulders, and began to weep into his hands. I didn't know what to do.

"She'll be all right," I said. But I knew better. Above the sound of the pump there was the beep of the heart monitor. Her heart was beating slowly and irregularly.

Sam turned back to me. His eyes were red and his face was streaked with tears. "I'm sorry, Jacob—they don't expect her to live through the night. There's too much damage."

A shiver ran through me. This isn't my mother. It can't be. I saw her this morning before I left for school. She has a meeting to go to tomorrow night. I touched her hand. It didn't feel like my mom's.

A nurse came in and checked the bottles and the monitors, then wrote something down on a clipboard.

"I'll have someone bring chairs," she said, then added gently to Sam, "Would you like a priest?"

Sam and I stared at her. *This isn't my mother! Chairs and a priest?*

"I don't think so," Sam said. "I don't know. Jacob, do you think . . ."

"No," I said. "We never went to church."

"Sometimes it's a comfort anyway," the nurse said.

"I think we'll be all right," Sam said.

She nodded and left the room.

We sat with her for the next seven hours. We didn't speak. There was nothing to say. At ten after three in the morning the heart monitor's beeping was replaced by a steady tone.

"Oh my God," Sam said.

The room filled with doctors and nurses.

Sam and I stood in stunned silence as they tried to get her back. Finally one of the doctors shook his head and reached over and flipped the heart monitor off. The room became quiet. I stared at my mom. Then I felt something on the back of my neck as if someone had brushed up against me, but when I turned my head to look no one was there.

My mom was gone.

Two

The funeral was on Sunday in a small chapel at the cemetery. Well over a hundred people were there to say good-bye. My mother would have liked that. She loved people and crowds.

After the service we walked by the open coffin. I looked at her for a long time. The bandages were gone now, and she looked peaceful, but nothing like she had looked in life. I kissed her on the forehead and walked out into the lobby, then through the glass doors outside. I didn't want to talk to anyone.

After the funeral several people came back to our apartment. They milled around, eating the catered food and talking quietly. I wanted to be alone, but Sam said that I should stick around and talk with people. *"Jacob, they're here to honor your mother and to be here for us."* I suppose he was right but I still wanted to be alone.

I stood by the window in the living room watching my mother's friends and wishing my father was with me. I needed him! We tried to reach him by cable and phone, but he was out in the field and no one knew when he would be back or even exactly where he was. He would have been here if he had known.

The front door opened and Bill Brewster, a friend of my dad's, strode into the room. It had been at least two years since I had seen him. When he entered, the room grew quiet. He was a tall good-looking guy with long shaggy hair. He wore blue jeans and a red Gortex coat. He was a field biologist and looked out of place among so many university professors. He reminded me of my father, who never looked quite right in our apartment or in the city. But put him in the woods, and he looked like an old tree that had always been there. My spirit lifted somewhat when he came in.

Sam walked over to him and shook his hand, and the talk started again. He talked to Sam for a moment, then he spotted me and came over.

"Sorry to hear about your mom," he said uncomfortably.

"Thanks."

He looked around the room. "I don't think I know anyone here."

"Friends of my mom and Sam's. Mostly from the university."

"Where's your dad?"

"He's out in the field, and we weren't able to reach him."

"Really?"

"Nobody seems to know where his camp is. They tried to reach him by radio, but there was no response."

"I'm not surprised," Bill said. "He's in a pretty remote area, and he moves around a lot."

"Do you know where he is?"

"I was in his new study area a couple of months ago. I imagine that he's still in the same general vicinity."

I was excited by the news. "Could you show me?"

"Sure," Bill said. "Do you have a map?"

I nodded and led him down the hall to my bedroom, where I had an entire wall of topographical maps of Kenya. Whenever my father wrote a letter about where he was I marked it on the map. It helped me to feel connected to him. Sometimes I'd stare at the maps and calculate what time it was in Kenya and imagine what my father might be doing at that moment.

"I'm impressed," Bill said, looking at the wall. "You've got better maps than your dad does." He turned to the opposite wall, which was covered with photos my father had sent me. "Your dad was always photo happy." He walked over to the wall and pointed at a photo of me with a tranquilizer rifle at the zoo with my dad.

"I remember this," he said. "Didn't he let you dart a couple of fallow deer for him that day?"

I nodded.

"Yeah, I remember. You made a good shot, and he was proud as hell about that." He laughed. "It's ironic. A lot of fathers are proud of their sons when they kill their first deer, but your dad was proud when you immobilized one."

I remembered it, too. It was one of my best moments with my dad. "He got in trouble for it," I said.

"That's an understatement!" Bill said. "The zoo almost fired him. They frown on twelve year olds darting their animals. Your father didn't give a damn, though. He was crazy then and he still is."

When Sam said my father was crazy, it made me angry. When Bill said it, it made me happy.

Bill walked over to the photo of my father and him in Kenya working on a tranquilized elephant.

"I remember this tusker," he said. "A dinosaur! Look at the ivory on him!"

My father was attaching a radio collar around the elephant's neck while Bill measured the tusks.

"The whole herd had big ivory," Bill went on excitedly. "Poachers have taken most of the big tuskers; these are some of the only ones left." He looked at me sadly. "Of course they're probably gone now. When I left, the poachers had the run of the country—it was driving your dad nuts."

"How is my dad?"

"He's okay, I guess." Bill walked over to the map and studied it for a moment, then turned back to me. "Like I was saying, things are bad in Kenya. The drought has really screwed up the country. There's no food, the coffee crop failed, and tourism is way down because of crime. In some parts of the country there have even been border skirmishes. The drought is worse in Somalia and Uganda. The people are crossing the borders in droves. It's a mess."

"What about my dad?" Something was up. Bill wasn't telling me everything.

"Your dad's pretty damn stubborn. The most pig-headed man I've ever known. He refused to leave when things got bad. His airplane is down, and he's been waiting for parts for months. He's been radio-tracking elephants from the ground—not easy to do. The institute is pulling out until things cool down. I'm surprised they answered the phone when you called. He's one of the few foreign biologists left in the bush."

"Is he going to be all right?"

Bill shrugged his shoulders. "It's hard to say. He's pretty much on his own now. To tell you the truth,

Jake, one of the reasons I came here today was to see if he pulled out. I was hoping he'd be here."

I wished he was here, too—now more than ever. "Is he in danger?"

"I don't know. There are a lot of bad things going on there. The military is spread pretty thin trying to keep a lid on things. They're concentrating their men in and around the cities, where the people are going. The bush is wide open, and the poachers know it."

"Where is he?" I pointed to the map.

"I don't know exactly, but—"

"Jacob?"

I turned and saw Sam standing in the open doorway. He looked irritated.

Sam stepped into the room. "What are you doing?" he asked.

"Talking to Bill."

"I see that."

"I was just telling him about his dad," Bill said.

Sam ignored him. "Well, Jacob, we have people here. Some of them would like to talk to you before they leave."

"Okay," I said. "I'll be out soon."

"Well, don't be too long," he said, and left.

I was embarrassed.

Bill looked at me sympathetically. "Maybe you should—"

"No," I said. "I want to know where my father is."

He turned back to the map. "I can't say for sure, but I can point out the general area where we were working. It's near the Tanzanian border, about here." He pointed to an area called the Nguruman Escarpment.

14

Three

The morning after the funeral, when I came into the kitchen, Sam was sitting at the table waiting for me.

"We've got to talk, Jacob," he said.

I sat down across from him. The first few days after my mom died Sam was different—we seemed to connect with each other—but now things were the same as before. I was angry at the way he had treated me after the funeral. We were uncomfortable now and awkward with each other.

"We've got to talk about the arrangements," he said.

"What arrangements?"

"What we're going to do." He played with his coffee mug.

I'd been so preoccupied with thoughts of my mom and the funeral that I hadn't even thought about what we were going to do.

"Your mom's folks aren't in a position to take you," he continued. "But I talked with your aunt and uncle in Nebraska—"

"What?" What did he mean—*take me*?

"Now hold on," he said. "They've offered to put you up. There's a high school right down the street."

"Nebraska?"

"It's not so bad there. They're a nice family."

"Why can't I just stay here and finish school?"

15

"You're making this difficult, Jacob."

I glared at him. I was making it difficult?

"You can't stay here," he said.

"Why?"

"Because I'm not going to be here. I need some time. A few weeks ago I was offered a position on a dig in Honduras. Of course, I told them that I couldn't take it. But things are different now."

"You're going to Honduras?"

He nodded. "I need time," he repeated. "With your mom gone, I just don't think I can stay here."

Nebraska? There had to be some other way. I had been there a couple of times, and there were problems. *Beth, your boy is wild. What he needs is some good old-fashioned discipline.* My uncle was beyond strict. My cousins, Wanda and Myron, were like terrified robots.

"I don't think my mom would have liked this arrangement," I said. "I don't get along with them. I'm surprised they even want me there."

"Well, they do," he said. "And it's the only alternative."

"What about my dad?"

"What about him?"

"Don't you think we should contact him before you make any decisions? He's my legal guardian now."

"I tried to contact him!" he shouted. "He didn't even come to Beth's funeral!"

"He would have if he had known," I shouted back.

Sam stood up angrily. "Your father's never given a damn about you or Beth!"

"That's not true!" I yelled. And it wasn't true. He wrote and called when he could. Even after my mom

16

married Sam, my dad continued to send support checks to my mom and money for me to put into my savings account.

"The hell it isn't," Sam said. "You're going to your cousins' and that's it! It's all been arranged."

"I want to wait until I hear from my father."

"There's no time. As soon as I can get things packed and sold, I'll be leaving."

"What do you mean sold?"

"We've got to do something with all this stuff. I won't be needing it where I'm going and neither will you."

"You're going to sell my mom's things?" I couldn't believe it. We just buried her the day before.

"What else am I supposed to do with them?"

"How about putting them in storage?"

"There's no point in that. And if it's the money you're worried about, don't. I plan to send a check to you as soon as everything's settled."

"Money?" I was devastated. "It's not the money."

"Then what is it?"

"It's my mom's stuff," I said.

"Oh." He sat down. "I'm sorry, Jacob," he said quietly. "I don't know what's gotten into me. This has been very hard on me. I'm not myself."

He was being himself. He just didn't know it.

"Of course, you can take anything you want to remember your mom by. But there isn't much room where you're going."

"Why can't I just stay here?"

"Because no one will be here to take care of you. Don't be ridiculous!" He stood up again. "You're lucky they offered to take you in."

Yeah, lucky me.

"I have to go to the university," Sam said. "We can talk about this later, but there's really nothing more to say."

Sam was right, there really was nothing more to say. After he left I went into my bedroom and looked at the photos on the wall. In each one, time was frozen for a moment. My mom at one of her digs holding an ancient piece of pottery she'd uncovered. My father holding an antenna in the air as he tracked elephants. Another of my father in his Land Rover in Africa. A photo of me graduating from the survival school that my mom and dad battled over for weeks. *"He's old enough, Beth. It's about time that he learned there is more to the world than asphalt, glass, and cement."* A photo of the three of us on a camping trip in Canada—all of us smiling—a long time ago.

I lay down on my bed. *"You can take anything you want to remember your mom by."* Thanks a lot—very kind of you. Just what do you *take* to remember your mom? It was obvious that the only thing that linked Sam and me was my mom's love for both of us. Now that she was gone, he was dumping me without considering for a second what I wanted. Not even waiting to hear from my father . . .

As my mind raged on I became more and more miserable. I was having a hard time breathing. I jumped out of bed, pushed the window open, and stuck my head outside. Pigeons flew off the ledge at the sound of the window banging open, and I took in big gulps of air. Below, people scurried past, unaware of my pain. I thought of jumping. That would certainly get their attention. They would know that I had been in pain. What was the matter with me? I'd never thought like this. I pulled my head back inside. Get a hold of yourself, Jake! I closed the window and quickly left the bedroom.

The living room was not much better. Everything there had been packed in boxes. The books, artifacts, and pictures. The things of my mom's life packed neatly away as if she had never existed.

I went into the kitchen. Sam hadn't gotten there with his boxes yet. My mom loved her kitchen. She got around in it pretty well. *"It's my domestic laboratory, and you are the guinea pigs."* Looking around the kitchen I began to feel hungry for the first time in days. The refrigerator was nearly empty. I opened the cupboard and found a can of soup. I opened it and poured the contents into a bowl, then opened the microwave to heat it. And there it was—the piece of lasagna. I took it out and put it on the kitchen table and sat down. Memories of my mom flooded back to me, and I began to cry. The tears came slowly at first. I remembered everything—wave after wave of things we had done together, her expressions, her laughter, things she had said. The grief billowed out of me, and I cried like I never had before.

Four

Sam and I didn't talk much over the next several days. He was preoccupied with preparations. He sorted through papers, packed boxes, and talked quietly on the phone. I went to school, checked the mailbox, and hung around, thinking that my father might call. But he didn't.

Sam came into my bedroom one night and said that he had to go out of town for a few days.

"An anthropology meeting in Chicago," he said. "When I get back we'll make the final arrangements for your trip to Nebraska." He handed me a stack of red tags. "Some people were here today to look at our things. Next week they'll take the stuff to auction. You'll need to pack your bedroom. Mark what you want to keep with these tags. It's a good time to get rid of the things you don't really use. Make a clean slate of it."

Early the next morning he left for his trip.

I didn't say good-bye, nor did he. From the bedroom I heard the door shut, then looked out the window and watched him climb into the back of a taxicab.

I made breakfast and got ready for school. On the hallway table, Sam had left me three twenties and a note.

Jacob,
This ought to cover your food while I'm gone.
Don't forget to pack.
                                                    Sam

Very warm, Sam. I pocketed the money and left for school.

Halfway there I stopped my bike. What was the point? In a couple of weeks I'd be in Nebraska and have to finish the school year there.

I decided to ride over to Central Park and use my pass to get into the zoo. *"The best time to visit the zoo is in the morning. The animals are more active. More themselves . . ."* My father had helped design several of the exhibits in the zoo. We used to spend a lot of time there together.

I wandered around looking at the animals. He was right—without a throng of people watching them, the animals seemed to move around more naturally. The polar bears were gliding through the water. The birds seemed at ease, their calls echoing as they flew through the tropical house. Because of my father, I knew most of the animals' scientific names. *"Animals have common names and secret names."* It was a game we played when I was younger. Polar bears were *Ursus maritimus*. Golden lion tamarins were *Leontopithecus rosalia*. The leaf-nosed bats they had were *Phyllostomidae carollia*.

I loved the zoo, and when my father worked there I would visit every day after school. My father had mixed feelings about the zoo. I think he worked there because it was the closest he could come to wildlife in New York City.

"There's nothing the matter with zoos, Jake. They're a good thing, but we sometimes get so focused on taking care of the animals that we forget why we have them. Each animal should tell a story about what is happening to it in the wild. If we fail in that, then we have no right to keep them in cages."

The zoo exhibits didn't look like cages. They looked natural, with plants, rocks, pools, and streams. None of the exhibits had bars to keep the animals in. Instead, they used hidden moats, glass, and thin, almost invisible, wire.

"They're still cages, Jake. No matter how pretty we make them, a cage is a cage. We all live in cages of one kind or another. Some are spacious and have everything a person could want. Others are small and have hardly anything in them—barely enough to get by. The big difference between cages are the barriers that keep us in them. Poverty, wealth, religion, hatred, jealousy, bitterness, responsibility, addiction—these are the bars that keep us locked in the cages. There are times when we are free to break through the barriers, but we rarely do. We grow comfortable in our cages—they're all we know."

After walking through the zoo I got back on my bike and rode through the park. It was overcast, but not raining. People sat on benches, joggers ran along the paths. An old woman muttered to herself as she pushed a shopping cart stuffed with everything she owned.

Some of the walls were covered with brightly colored graffiti. *"To me, this is the only true art of our century. In a few thousand years anthropologists like your mother will be trying to figure out what these paintings mean. Modern cave paintings, twenty-first-century petroglyphs."*

When I got home the mailman was stuffing letters into the apartment's mailbox.

"Do you have anything for Lansa?" I asked.

"Sure do," he said, and handed me a short stack of mail.

I recognized the letter from my father right away.

It was in a Wildlife Research Institute envelope, and like the last few letters I had received from him, it was taped as if it had been opened and resealed. I didn't want to read it in the lobby. I wheeled my bike into the elevator and punched the button for our floor.

I went into the apartment and sat on the couch. The letter was dated two weeks before my mother died.

February 18

Jake,

This is probably going to be the last letter you get for a while. In fact, I hope you get this letter. I hear there's been some problem with the mail lately.

The drought has all but ruined the country. Poachers are slaughtering the animals. They're using sophisticated weapons and equipment, and they're backed by big money. People are starving to death and dying of AIDS.

The institute is probably going to close down, though we need to be here—now more than ever! If we pull out, there may be nothing to come back to.

I'm going to stay on as long as I can, but I don't want you or your mother to worry. I'm perfectly fine out here. The rains will come eventually, and when they do, many of the problems will be washed away. This is not the first or last time a drought has been here. The difference now is that there are more people here then ever before. There's simply not enough food to go around.

I'm making this short so I can get it on the truck going to Nairobi. Again, don't worry about me. I'll write when I can.

All my love,
Dad

I read the letter several times. Each time through I tried to imagine what he was leaving out. *"Look at the white space, Jake. The blanks. Sometimes it's the things we can't see and don't hear that are the most important."* My father repeated this often, and for years it was a meaningless riddle to me. But I had learned that there might be something to it. *"Listen carefully to the words people are saying, then later go back over what they said and try to imagine what they didn't say and ask yourself why they left these things out."* This took a lot of time, and I had to really concentrate, but when I took the time to see and hear what wasn't there, I reached a deeper understanding. Dad was right about that.

The white space of my father's letter told me that he was frustrated and angry. I had seen him this way many times. My mother understood him. *"He's in one of his moods. I guess we can be thankful he's a biologist and not a policeman. He would think nothing of step-ping in front of a bullet to save someone."* And when he was in one of his moods he did rash things. I was very worried about him. But what could I do? My only hope was that he would get the message we had left about my mom and come back to the States.

Still holding the letter, I picked up the phone and dialed the Wildlife Research Institute in Kenya. It took a long time to connect.

"Jambo." A man answered.

"Hi, I'm trying to reach Dr. Robert Lansa."

"Who?"

"Robert Lansa."

"Yes. Yes. One moment, please."

There was the muffled sound of people speaking in the background.

"Hello?" A woman's voice. She sounded American. I was disappointed—for a moment I thought my dad actually might be there.

"This is Jacob Lansa," I said. "I'm looking for my father."

"I know," the woman said. It must have been the same woman Sam had spoken to before my mom's funeral. "We're looking for him, too. Unfortunately we haven't been able to find him. He's out in the bush."

"Is he all right?"

"I think so," she said. "I mean . . . I'm sure he's fine. We've lost communication with the area he's in. We're trying to get word to him."

"When do you think you might be able to reach him?"

"It's hard to say," she said. "We'll keep trying."

"I heard that the institute was closing down."

She hesitated. "Well that's true, but we'll be back when things get better here."

"What about my father?"

Again she hesitated before answering. "I'm sure he's gotten the word by now. He's probably tying up some loose ends and then he'll be in."

"Could you please tell him to call Jacob when he gets a chance?"

"Certainly."

"There's been a problem here and I need to talk to him."

"I understand. I was sorry to hear the news. He'll be in touch as soon as he can. Try not to worry."

"Thanks."

I hung up. *It's the things we can't see and don't hear that are the most important.* The woman was afraid. My father was in danger.

I went into my bedroom and opened my desk drawer. I took out my savings account book and my passport. I had gotten the passport three years ago for a trip to Sweden with my mom. I looked at the photograph. I looked a lot older now. I wouldn't need a passport in Nebraska, but I wasn't going to Nebraska.

Five

That afternoon I went to the library and checked out all the books I could find about Kenya. I stopped at a map store and bought more detailed maps of the route I would take to the Nguruman Escarpment. I skimmed the books and looked closely at the maps. I took notes and wrote a list of the things that I needed to do before I left.

Sam was coming back in three days. It would be much easier if I could leave before he returned.

That night I didn't go to sleep until well after midnight. I was exhausted, but happy for the first time in days. In my mind, I wasn't running away. I didn't belong in Nebraska—I belonged with my father, no matter where he was. I didn't know how he would feel about this, and I didn't even know if I could find him. But I had to try.

The next morning I turned on my mom's computer and wrote a letter to the Kenyan Embassy.

To whom it may concern:
    I am requesting a visa for my son, Jacob Lansa. His mother passed away on March 3. I am working in Kenya as a field biologist for the Wildlife Research Institute.
    Because of his mother's death, I would like Jacob to join me here until we can work out other arrangements.
    I have sent him an air ticket to Kenya. At this

time I am asking for a tourist visa. Should we decide to prolong his stay, we will apply for a long-term visa with the proper authorities.

I am currently working in the field and it is difficult to reach me by phone,

I hesitated. This was the risky part. If I gave his phone number, the embassy might call the institute. I didn't know what they would say about my coming over there. The plan could be shattered in a second. And what if my father was back from the field? What if he was at the institute offices? It would be embarrassing, but at least I'd be able to talk to him.

I continued:

but you can try.
The number is: 27047 331 866. I would like to get Jacob over here as soon as possible, as he has no one to take care of him in New York.
Thank you for your assistance in this matter.
Sincerely,
Dr. Robert Lansa

Not too bad. I found some institute stationery and printed the letter out, then forged my father's signature.

As I was reading the letter over, I was startled by the phone ringing. I picked it up.

"Jacob?" It was Sam.

"Hi." Great timing. Stupidly, I flipped the letter over—as if he could see it. I almost laughed.

"How's it going?"

"Fine."

"Look," he said. "There are some things I need to take care of here. Do you think you'd be okay for a few more days?"

A miracle. "Sure," I said eagerly.

"What's the matter?"

Too eager.

"Nothing," I said. "Why?"

"I don't know," Sam said. "You just sound in much better spirits."

"I guess I am," I said.

"How's the money holding out?"

"Fine."

"Good," he said. "I should be back within a week. Could you do me a favor?"

"Sure."

"Call the auction company. The number's by the phone. Tell them that I'm out of town, and we'll have to reschedule the pickup. Tell them I'll call when I get back."

"Are you still going to Honduras?"

"Yeah," he said. "In fact, it's the arrangements that are delaying me here. I have to interview potential student assistants for the trip."

I didn't say anything.

"Anyway," he continued. "I better be going. Everything okay?"

"Sure," I said. "Everything's fine."

"Good. Well, I'll call you later this week."

I hung up the phone. He acted like nothing had happened. It was like my mother hadn't died. *Look for what isn't there.* Perhaps he was throwing himself into this new job as a way of dealing with his grief. It didn't matter—by the time he got back I would be in the African bush. Before his call I was feeling somewhat guilty about what I was about to do, but now what little guilt I had was gone. I wondered if Sam would even notice that I wasn't here when he returned.

Six

My first stop was the bank. I had eighteen hundred dollars in my savings account. I withdrew it all and closed the account.

The next stop was a travel agency. I locked my bike outside and walked in.

"How can I help you?" the woman at the counter asked.

"I need a ticket to Nairobi, Kenya."

"Really? Come on back and we'll see what we can do."

I followed her over to her desk and sat down. This was the first time I had ever done anything like this and I was a little nervous, but if she noticed she didn't seem to care.

"I'll need your name and address."

I gave it to her, and she typed it into her computer.

"When would you like to leave?"

"On the thirteenth," I said.

"In two days?"

"Right."

"That's short notice," she said. "It's going to be expensive."

I wasn't worried—I had eighteen hundred bucks in my pocket.

"When will you be returning?" she asked.

"I don't know," I said.

"You want an open ticket then?"

"I guess."

"This is really going to cost a lot," she said, typing more information into the computer. "There's a flight leaving at 8:00 P.M. from Kennedy on the thirteenth."

"That'll be fine," I said. "How much is it?"

"Let's see. It comes to $1,964."

"How much?" I was shocked.

She repeated the price. I didn't have that much money and I still needed to buy some things for the trip, besides having money for expenses when I got there.

"Is that the best price?"

"I'm afraid so," she said. "On such short notice that's the best we can do."

"What about a one-way ticket?"

"That's less," she said. "But not a lot less. And Kenya won't give you a visa on a one-way ticket. They want to make sure that you have transportation back out of the country."

I didn't know what to do. I thought I would have plenty of money. The plan was falling apart. The woman looked at me, waiting for me to say something.

"I guess I'll have to wait," I said.

"Fine," she said. "There are plenty of seats. People aren't going to Kenya these days. You know there's a drought there, and the word we're getting is that the country isn't all that safe."

"Yeah, I heard." I got up from the chair. "I appreciate your help."

"My pleasure." She stood up. "Why are you going to Kenya?"

"To see my father."

"Well, perhaps he can send you the money."

"Yeah," I said, walking out of the office.

I unlocked my bike, got on, and started back to the apartment. It was over before it began. Nice try, Jake! It looked like I was going to spend the next few years in Nebraska.

I pedaled along slowly, trying to think of a way to get the money. As I rode, I saw a row of pawnshops across the street. I crossed over and stopped in front of one of them. The barred window was filled with musical instruments, cameras, stereo equipment, and jewelry. *"Take anything you want to remember your mom by."* She would have approved. I rode back to the apartment as fast I could pedal.

Inside, I went directly to my mother's bedroom. I hadn't been in there since she died. Sam had, though. Boxes filled with my mom's clothes covered the floor. On top of her dresser was her jewelry box.

I picked up the box and poured the contents onto the bed. Among the jewelry was a very old amulet that Taw had given to my father and my father had given to my mother. It was made out of a round flat stone, about the size of a quarter. There was a hole in the middle and surrounding the hole was an intricately carved snake swallowing its tail. A leather thong was strung through the hole so that it could be worn as a necklace.

I looked at it for a long time. The amulet had been important to my parents and to Taw. I slipped it over my head and put it under my shirt. Having it against my chest seemed to make me feel better. It was as if my parents were close to me again.

In the pile of jewelry I found my mom's diamond engagement and wedding rings—the ones my father had given her. I also found the gold necklace with a small emerald that my mother's grandmother had given her. *"They're worth a fortune, but I wouldn't sell them for the world."* I put the necklace and the rings in my pocket and left the apartment.

I had never been inside a pawnshop, but I had a pretty good idea of how they worked. You gave them something of value, and they gave you a fraction of what it was worth and a pawn ticket as a receipt. If you didn't buy your stuff back within a certain amount of time, then they sold it.

I was the only customer. The things inside were all behind wire mesh—I guess to keep people from stealing them. As I walked up to the counter, I felt like I was an animal in the zoo, or maybe the pawnbroker was the animal.

A man was sitting in a small office in the back watching television.

"Excuse me," I said.

He got up from his chair very slowly and walked over to the counter. He was very tall and his hair was braided in long dreadlocks.

"What do you have?" he asked.

"Some jewelry," I said.

"Let's see it."

I put the rings and the necklace on the counter and he scooped them through the slot in the wire mesh. He took out a jeweler's magnifying glass and looked at the rings, then he held the necklace under a bright light and examined it closely.

"I'll give you a hundred dollars," he said.

"For all of them?"

"Yeah, for all of them."

A hundred dollars wouldn't do me any good.

"They're worth a lot more than that," I said.

"Not to me," he said, and pushed them back through the slot.

I thought about it for a moment. Nineteen hundred dollars wouldn't even pay for the airplane tickets—there wasn't any point. Nice try, Jake. I picked up the things and turned to go.

"Wait a second," the pawnbroker said. "Let me see those again."

I turned and put them back on the counter. He pulled them back through the slot and looked at them again.

"Where'd you get these things?"

"My mom," I said. "She died."

"Yeah, right," he said sarcastically.

"She did!" I felt anger well up inside.

"When?"

I took a deep breath.

"On March third," I said quietly.

The pawnbroker looked at me for a moment. "When was the funeral?"

"Sunday."

"What's your name?"

"Why?"

"So I can check the obits."

"Obits?"

"The obituaries," he said. "I've got to make sure these things aren't hot."

"I didn't steal them," I said, trying to control my anger.

"Well, in our business you can never be too sure. I gotta check. What was her name?"

"Beth Walters," I said.

He went back into his office, and I heard him rummaging around. After a moment he came back holding a newspaper.

"And what's your name?"

"Jacob."

He read from the newspaper: "She is survived by her husband, Samuel Walters, and her son, Jacob Lansa."

He put the newspaper down. "Does your father know that you're doing this?"

"They're not his," I said.

"I see," he said. "I'll give you two hundred dollars."

"No," I said. That would get me the ticket but I wouldn't have any money left. "This isn't going to work. Just give me the stuff back."

He looked at me. "What's that around your neck?"

The amulet was dangling outside of my shirt. "Just something from my dad."

"Can I see it?"

"It's not for sale," I told him.

"I didn't say I wanted to buy it," he said. "I just want to look at it."

I didn't see any harm in his looking at it. I took it off and handed it through the slot. He looked at it under the magnifying glass, then looked back at me.

"I'll give you three hundred for everything, including this."

I thought about it for a moment. But something wasn't right. Something happened to me when I took the amulet off. I felt strange, uncomfortable.

"No," I said. "It's not for sale." I put my hand out.

"Do you know what this is?"

"Something my grandfather had," I said impatiently. "I'd like it back now."

"It's very old," he said. His attitude seemed to have softened a little. "It's a powerful symbol, but it has no real value."

"It does to me," I said, still holding out my hand.

He laughed. "I can see that," he said looking at the amulet again. "I'll tell you what I'll do. I'll give you three hundred for the necklace and the ring." He handed the amulet back to me. I quickly put it back around my neck, and as soon as I did, I felt better. What was going on here? How could a piece of carved stone make me feel better? Magic? I remembered a disagreement my mom and dad had.

"All magic can be explained in scientific terms."

"I don't think so, Beth. Literature is filled with examples of unexplained magic."

"That's right, Bob—literature is fiction."

"Then why do the stories endure?"

"Because people want to believe in miracles. It's why millions of people buy lottery tickets every day."

"Well, how about it?" The pawnbroker asked, startling me.

"Three hundred?"

"I shouldn't even offer you that much," he said. "My boss isn't going to be happy."

I thought about it. It wouldn't give me much money after I bought the ticket. With Sam's sixty and what I could scrape up around the house, I would have only about two hundred to take with me to Africa, but it might work.

"Okay," I said reluctantly.

He filled out the tickets and handed them to me. "Look, kid," he said kindly. "I don't know what you need the money for, but you have six months to redeem these tickets to get your mother's things back. Don't lose the tickets. I have a feeling that you're going to want these things back."

He was right about that.

I rode back to the travel agency and bought the airline tickets, and from there I went to the Kenyan Embassy to see about getting a visa.

"I need a visa," I said to the woman sitting at the information desk.

"Do you have a passport?"

I handed her my passport, and she looked at it very carefully, then back at me. "How old are you?"

"Fourteen."

"You need your parents' permission."

"I have that," I said, and handed her the letter I'd written.

She read the letter. "I see," she said, without saying anything about my mother dying. "Room thirty-nine," she said. "By the elevators." She handed the letter and passport back to me.

My father had written to me about Kenyan bureaucracy. *They make American bureaucrats look like amateurs. It's a religion to them, and they relish making you squirm with their squirts of power.* I walked over to the door and knocked lightly.

"Come in."

Sitting behind a large desk was an equally large man wearing a three-piece suit. He smiled when I came in.

"Please sit down," he said slowly, motioning me

to the chair across from his desk.

"You want to go to Kenya?"

"Yes," I said.

"When?"

"On the thirteenth."

He looked mildly surprised. "Of this month?"

"Yes."

"We don't usually issue visas so quickly."

I felt the plan coming apart again. "I need to meet my father there," I said.

"I see," he said.

I handed him the passport and the letter.

"What's this?" he asked, holding the folded letter.

"It's from my father."

He read the letter slowly, then looked at me. "I am very sorry to hear about your mother."

"Thanks," I said.

"So you have no one to take care of you in New York?"

"Not really," I said.

"Your father is a field biologist?"

"Yes."

He looked at me for a while without saying anything, which made me more nervous than I already was. I started to sweat and hoped he wouldn't notice.

"At the Wildlife Research Institute?"

"Yes."

He carefully went through a stack of papers on his desk until he found the one he was looking for. He read the paper carefully.

"This memo tells me that the Wildlife Research Institute has closed down."

I didn't know what to say. I felt like running out of

his office. "I know," I said. "But my father is still working there."

"I see," he said. "Do you have airline tickets?"

"Yes."

"May I see them, please?"

I handed him the tickets. He took them out of the envelope and looked at them.

"Please wait here a moment," he said, then got up from the desk and left the office carrying the letter, my passport, and the airline tickets.

He had everything, so there wasn't any point in running, although I still felt like it. I wondered if I would be able to cash the tickets back in. It didn't look like I was going to get a visa, and I couldn't get into the country without one.

On the wall behind the desk was a large color photo of Daniel arap Moi, the president of Kenya. It was a smaller version of the same photo in the embassy lobby. The night before, I had read that Moi had been in office since 1978, the year that Jomo Kenyatta died. Kenyatta became president in 1963 after four years of brutal fighting to win independence from Britain.

The door opened behind me, and the man came in and sat back down.

"I will have to call the Wildlife Research Institute," he said.

It's over, I thought. He picked up the phone and dialed the institute's number in Kenya. He smiled at me as he waited for the connection.

"Hello? Yes, this is the Kenyan Embassy in New York. I am looking for Dr. Robert Lansa."

"Yes. Is he there? Do you know when he'll be

back? I see. . . . I see. . . . I have his son in my office, and he is applying for a visa. . . . I see. . . . I see. . . ."

I wished I knew what he was "seeing." This whole thing was driving me crazy.

"Yes. . . . I see. . . . I see. . . . Well, Jacob will be arriving in Nairobi on the evening of the fourteenth. Yes, that's right."

I was in! I couldn't believe it.

"Yes. . . . Okay. . . . Good-bye." He hung up the phone and looked at me. "I assume your father knows when you are arriving in Nairobi."

"Of course," I lied.

"Good," he said. "I think, because of the circumstances, we will be able to issue you a visa today." He reached into his drawer and took out a stamp and very carefully stamped my passport.

I took my things back and thanked him. I still couldn't believe it. Outside, I unlocked my bike and began the ride back to the apartment. It was nearly five in the evening, and people were pouring out of the buildings onto the street. I wanted to tell every one of them that I was going to Kenya. I was going to see my father.

Seven

When I got home I checked my list. Because of the money situation I'd have to modify the original plan. I wouldn't have money to stay in a hotel every night, and I wouldn't be able to afford to hire someone to drive me to the area my father was in. I called the travel agent.

"This is Jacob Lansa. I was wondering if it's possible to take my bike to Kenya."

"Your bike?"

"Yeah," I said. "My mountain bike."

She didn't answer right away. "I don't see why not. People take them to Europe all the time. But this is the first time that I've heard of someone wanting to take a bike to Africa."

"Would it cost more?"

"I don't think so," she said. "It depends on what else you're taking and how much room there is on the flight. Let me call the airline and ask them. Hold on a minute."

A while later she came back on the line. "They said it would be no problem. They'll put your bike in a cardboard container when you get to the airport."

"Great," I said, and hung up.

I took down the maps of Kenya and spread them on the living-room floor. The Nguruman Escarpment was about two hundred and fifty miles from Nairobi. I would be able to stay on the main road until I got to Ewaso Ngiro. After that I would ride south on the dirt road for about forty miles, then cut across the Lebetero Hills. I figured that I could ride thirty to forty miles a day on the paved road and maybe twenty miles a day on the dirt road. After that I didn't know what I was going to do.

At the wake, Bill had marked where he *thought* my father's camp was. "And he's always breaking camp and moving it," he said. "If he stays in one place too long people show up asking if they can do odd jobs in exchange for food. It's hard to turn them away—they're starving, and there's no place for them to go. At one point he had nearly a hundred people staying around his camp. He finally arranged for them to be moved to the nearest refugee camp. Of course, the refugee camps are grim places, but at least there's a little bit of food trickling into them and some medical help."

The only thing I could hope for was to get to the general area, then ask for specific directions. Providing there was someone to ask. I marked my route on the map and figured on eight or nine days to get there.

I packed my gear. Sleeping bag, drop cloth, compass, binoculars, water bottles, knife, matches, cooking utensils, small camp stove, bicycle tools, tire pump, tire repair kit, sweater, two shirts, two pairs of jeans, jacket, baseball cap, T-shirts, underwear, socks, and a set of bicycle panniers to carry everything in.

I was confident that I'd be all right, despite the drought. I had done very well in the summer survival course in Arizona. I knew how to find water, get a fire going without matches, find food, read a map, use a compass, and build a shelter.

"Survival in the wilderness is a matter of keeping

your head. You've got to realize that time is different when you're in a survival situation. It can take you a whole day to find water, build a fire, and make a shelter. You've just got to realize that you are not going to cover as much ground as you normally would. Survival eats your time up, and if you ignore this principle you'll get eaten up. Survival is more important than getting there."

Remembering what the instructor said, I modified my estimate from nine days to fourteen days. *"Survival is more important than getting there."*

The next morning I rode to the outdoor store and bought packets of freeze-dried food and camp-stove fuel. The food was expensive but lightweight and it wouldn't take up too much room. Beef Stroganoff, eggs, chicken, soups, and vegetables. When I got back to the apartment I packed and repacked my panniers several times. I wasn't taking much with me, but it was still a lot for the small bags.

Then I took my loaded bike out for a test ride through Central Park. I jumped curbs, sped along the asphalt paths, cut through bushes, and rode over the grass and along dirt trails. The extra weight slowed me down, and it was more difficult to maneuver with the bulky panniers over the rear wheels, but overall I felt good about the ride.

The only thing I had to do before taking off for Kenya was visit Taw. Sam wanted to tell him about my mom over the phone, but I insisted that we tell him in person. Taw was fond of my mom, and I wanted to be there when he heard that she was gone. He was in a nursing home near Poughkeepsie. I planned to leave early the next morning, which would give me plenty of time to get back and catch my flight that evening.

Back in the apartment, I took my helmet off and leaned my loaded bike against the wall. I was very happy and very hungry. I couldn't really afford it, but I decided to order dinner from Chin's Kitchen. My last dinner in New York.

I walked into the living room and froze. Sam was sitting on the couch, talking on the phone. He smiled when I came in and held up his index finger indicating that he would be off the phone soon.

"Right," he said into the phone. "That's what I was saying. . . ."

I quickly backed out of the room, grabbed my helmet and bike, and left the apartment. What was he doing home? I thought about leaving right then—just hanging around somewhere until my plane left, but Sam might come looking for me. I wheeled the bike down the hall and into the elevator. I had a key to our storage closet in the basement. My bike panniers would be safe there until I decided what I was going to do. I took them off, then wheeled the bike back into the elevator.

Before going up, I stopped in the lobby and got our mail. Nothing from my father, but I hadn't expected anything.

When I got to the apartment I took a deep breath before I opened the door. I put my bike in the hallway. Sam was off the phone, sitting on the living-room floor sorting through papers.

"What happened to you?" he asked.

"I went down and got the mail." I handed him the pile. "I thought you weren't coming back for a few days," I said casually.

"Well I wasn't," he said. "But the student interviews went better than I expected. I was able to pick my assistants out of the first batch. And I have so much to do here."

"Right," I said.

"I see you've been sorting through your things," he said pointing to the camping gear spread out on the floor.

I hadn't put away the things I wasn't going to use.

"Yeah," I said, still in shock.

"What are you up to?"

"I thought I'd just pack some things," I said. "Maybe order some takeout from Chin's."

"Great idea," he said cheerfully. "I'm starving to death. That airplane food is hardly edible."

"Well, what do you want?"

"Anything will do," he said. "Here, my treat." He handed me a twenty.

I left my bike in the apartment and walked the block to Chin's. It gave me a chance to think about what I was going to do now. Within twenty-four hours I was supposed to be on a flight for Kenya. I could just see it now.

Sam: So what do you have going?
Me: Oh I don't know, I thought I'd fly to Africa tomorrow.
Sam: Cool. Make sure you clean your room before you go.
Me: No problem.

I picked up the food and walked back to the apartment. Sam ate while he sorted through papers and packed boxes. He talked excitedly about his new job in Honduras, the new students, the paper he had given at the meeting. He didn't mention my mother once. *The blank spaces . . .* He *had* to be throwing himself into his work to avoid dealing with the tragedy of my mother's death—there was no other explanation for his apparent happiness.

"I need to see Taw," I said. "Before I go to Nebraska."

"Really?"

"He doesn't know about Mom yet."

"That's right." The mention of my mom changed his attitude—a little. "When are you thinking of going?"

"Tomorrow," I said.

"Shoot," he said, snapping his fingers. "I can't make it tomorrow."

Who said anything about your going, Sam? He hated visiting my grandfather. The last time Sam had come with us, Taw had mistaken him for my father. Sam wasn't too happy about that.

"I didn't expect you to go," I said. "In fact, I was going to spend the weekend with him."

"The weekend? Where will you stay?"

"At the retirement home. They have a room visitors can stay in. I've done it before." I hadn't done it before, but they did let people stay there.

"I don't know, Jacob."

"It's my last chance to see him before I go."

He thought about it. "I guess it will be all right," he finally said. "How will you get there?"

"The train," I said. "I'm going to take my bike with me, so I'll have something to do when he takes his nap."

"Well," Sam said, looking through a folder. "Say hello to him for me."

"Sure." I stood up and stretched. "I'm going to bed. Good night."

Sam was busy sorting through papers and didn't even respond.

Eight

I didn't sleep very well. At about four in the morning I got out of bed, dressed, and quietly left the apartment without waking Sam.

Going to see Taw had been on my mind for a long time. A week before my mom died, I had asked her if we could see him. *"Of course! As soon as I have a free weekend."* I would have plenty of time to go up there and come back before my plane left. It was either that or spend the day at the airport.

Before Taw went to the convalescent home he lived by himself in a small apartment in the Bronx. When I was younger I spent quite a bit of time with him. He'd tell me about his childhood on the Hopi reservation in Arizona and take me up in skyscrapers he had worked on as a young man.

"It took us over three years to build this one. The winter was bad the year we got to the top. The wind blew in gusts and there was ice on the girders. We spent more time dangling from our safety ropes than we did walking on the steel. . . ."

And then his mind started to slip. He would wander away from his apartment and forget where he lived. They took him to the best doctors in New York, but they all said the same thing. *"He's an old man, there's nothing we can do to reverse that. You'll have to keep a close eye on him."* For a few months he lived with us, but it didn't work out. We had a two-bedroom apartment, and we couldn't afford a bigger one, which meant that he had to stay in my room. I didn't mind, but he had insomnia, and every night he would turn on the television and all the lights and wander around talking to himself. None of us slept.

Because my parents both worked, they had to leave him alone during the day. More often than not, they'd come home to find him gone. And the search would begin—my mother called police stations and hospitals, while my father and I walked the streets checking shelters, asking people if they had seen him. A couple of times we found that he'd been beaten up. Another time he had been hit by a car.

They found a place that would take him during the day—a day-care center for old people. Apparently Taw didn't like it. He managed to escape three or four times and eventually they said he couldn't stay there anymore.

My father wanted to take him back to Arizona, but the catch was that Taw wanted us to move, too, so we could be close to him. I was all for it, but my mother flatly refused. She didn't want to leave her position at the university—a position that she had worked very hard for.

Finally, my father put him in the home near Poughkeepsie, and luckily, Taw seemed to like it there. He hadn't once tried to wander away.

The train left for Poughkeepsie at 6:30. I carried my bike onto the train.

The train was nearly empty. Most people were

coming into the city, not leaving it. I found a window seat and got comfortable.

I pulled out the folder with all of my father's letters and photographs. I had taken them with me because I didn't want anything to happen to them in the move. I felt that they would be safe with Taw until I got back.

The letters my dad sent during the last year were much more personal than in previous years. They read like journal entries.

I think that the main reason I choose to study animals in the field is so I can be in wild places. I feel at home here.

Studying elephants is like going back into prehistoric times. In size, elephants are the closest things we have to dinosaurs. There are days when I feel as though there is nothing we can do for elephants—I feel that the only good I am doing is recording the extinction of one of the most magnificent animals that ever walked the earth.

We biologists don't talk much about how animals feel. It's not scientific. But after watching elephants all these years, I'm convinced that they feel strong emotions. All you have to do is watch a mother elephant with her calf. I believe that elephants are just as capable of love and grief as we are. . . .

The most recent letters were about the drought and how this was affecting the elephants and the people of Kenya.

The drought has made poaching very easy.

The animals must drink, and the poachers simply wait at the watering holes.

Most of the mature bull elephants have been killed for their ivory. To keep up with the demand for ivory, poachers now kill twice as many young bulls and cows. In 1970 there were 140,000 elephants in Kenya. Today there are less than 20,000. If this continues the elephant will be gone from Kenya by the end of the century.

The ban on ivory has doubled the price on the black market, making poaching a very profitable business. The poachers have no problem finding people to help with the killing. The people in the bush are so hungry that most of them help the poachers in exchange for meat from the fallen animal. The poachers provide the people with food, jobs, and money. It's hard for the people to resist.

Some poaching bands use automatic weapons to kill elephants. Others use arrows. They dip the arrows into a poisonous black tar. All they have to do is to get close enough to an elephant to put an arrow into it anywhere on its body. Once the arrow is placed, they wait. The poison acts on the nerves that control the heart. They simply follow the elephant until it collapses, and then they go to work. . . .

As I read through the letters I began to worry about my father's reaction to my coming to Africa. He had enough problems and might not want to deal with another one in the form of his son. When I found him, what if he put me back on an airplane bound for Nebraska?

Technology has brought us many wonderful

things, but I think that we have lost more than we have gained from these wonderful inventions. Technology allows us to take more from the land than we need—and this is often more than the land can bear. We can shoot all of the animals with guns, and take all of the nutrients out of the soil with chemicals. Trains and airplanes get us to places quicker so we can exploit those places. These inventions came so quickly that we didn't have time to develop an ethic for using them. I realize that technology is here to stay—but are we better off? Without technology we would have fewer options. But, with fewer options, perhaps we would be able to make better decisions.

Well, Dad, I thought, I may not be making the best decisions right now, but I'm very thankful for the options, because they are going to take me to you.

The train pulled into the Poughkeepsie station at about 8:30. I got on my bike and started for the retirement home. It was a beautiful morning with more blue sky than gray. It took me about an hour to ride to the home.

On nice days like today, Taw was usually outside. He had a special chair next to the small creek that ran in back of the home. He'd sit there for hours staring at the stream. I always wondered what he thought about while he sat there, what he saw during those long hours by the stream.

It had been at least six months since I'd seen him. I never knew what he was going to be like on these visits. Some days he remembered everything—my name, my mother, his name, and where he was. Other days, he had no idea what was going on. He jumped from one thing to another. One moment he was running around on the reservation with his childhood friends, the next moment he was on a skyscraper in New York talking with one of his buddies.

I walked my bike around back. There were about twenty people staying in the home. It looked like most of them were outside. Some of them were in wheelchairs, others sat around a picnic table where a nurse was calling out bingo numbers. A group of men sat at a card table playing poker. Others were working on craft projects—painting, needlework, and ceramics.

"Hey, Jake!" Peter, one of the orderlies, came trotting up to me. "I can't believe this!"

"Can't believe what?" I asked, leaning my bike against the fence.

"Your grandfather said that you were on your way here."

"He what?" I couldn't believe it, either.

"He said you were coming here," he said. "Did you call and tell him?"

"No."

"I didn't think so," he said. "I told him not to be disappointed if you didn't show. The old fart just smiled at me like I didn't know what I was talking about. I guess he was right."

There was no way Taw could have known—unless Sam had called. "Did my stepfather call?" I asked.

"Nope. Pretty weird!"

That was an understatement. I looked over toward the creek and saw my grandfather sitting in his usual spot, looking at the water, unaware that I'd arrived.

Peter looked at his watch. "He's going to be taking his nap soon. How about a game of chess when he does?"

Peter and I usually played chess when Taw napped.

"I'm kind of on a tight schedule," I said. "We'll see." The train for New York left at 3:19. I didn't want to miss it.

"Well, let me know," Peter said. "The board's set up in the office."

"Okay," I said, and walked over to Taw.

Not even my father knew exactly how old Taw was, but he was probably well into his eighties. His long white hair was unbraided and hung below his shoulders. Like my father, he was thin and wiry. He still looked strong, despite the fact that he hadn't done any physical labor in years.

"Hello, Taw!" I said cheerfully. He looked at me and smiled but didn't say anything. In a moment I'd be able to tell if he was going to be with me or not. He continued to look at me. "It's good to see you," I said.

"It's good to see you," he said. "I knew you were coming."

"That's what Peter said." But do you know who I am? I thought.

"He didn't believe me," he said.

"He believes you now."

Taw laughed, then looked back at the stream.

"I saw a fish rise," he said seriously. "The first I've seen in a long time. It was beautiful."

I thought I might as well see if he was with me. "There's been some problems at home," I said. He looked back at me. "My mom died a few days ago." As soon as I said it, a lump of grief rose in my throat. "An accident," I continued. "She was hit by a car while she was jogging. . . ."

When I imagined the car hitting my mother, the grief exploded out of me—I couldn't hold it back: I sank to my knees in front of Taw and put my head in his lap. As I sobbed, I felt his bony old hand stroking my head. His touch was a great comfort to me, but I kept on weeping for what seemed like a long time. When I was done I lifted my head and wiped the tears from my face.

"Sorry, Taw."

"Sorry?" he said. "Don't be sorry. Tears are the greatest thing you can leave for someone who has passed to the underworld. To be missed is all they have left here."

I looked at him. It was the first time I had ever heard him speak of the Hopi way. What I knew of the Hopi beliefs, I had gotten from my father. *The Hopi believe in life after death. The world they go to is like a mirror image of this world. When it is winter here it is summer there. When someone dies here someone is born in the underworld.* I had tried to get Taw to tell me about the Hopi ways many times, but he always changed the subject, like he wasn't interested in talking about it.

"Your mother was a good woman," he said. "I will miss her. She came to see me often."

It was true. Even after she and my father divorced she continued to visit. "How did you know I was coming?"

"I'm not sure," he said. "I just felt it."

"Have you ever felt this way before?"

"Not for a very long time," he said. "Many years ago I used to feel things—know things that were about to happen. Lately, some of these things have been coming back to me."

Taw was clearheaded. I was very happy I had come. "I don't have a lot of time," I said. "In a few hours I have to take the train back to New York."

"Back to Sam," he said.

I was surprised he remembered who Sam was. "Not exactly," I said. "Can you keep a secret?"

"All I have is secrets," he said.

"I'm going to Africa."

He looked off in the direction of the creek and didn't say anything for a long time. I thought that he might be drifting off. Then he turned back to me and said, "That explains it."

"Explains what?"

"The dream," he said. "Two nights ago I saw you walking in a big land. You were not alone, but I could not see who you were with."

"Was I riding my bike?"

He looked surprised. "No, you were walking."

"I'm taking my bike with me."

"To Africa?"

"To ride to Dad's camp."

He closed his eyes in concentration, then opened them again. "There was no bike, but it could have been there. These dreams are often incomplete."

"What else did you see?"

He thought a moment. "Nothing. It was very dry, very hot, and you were tired."

"What about Dad?"

"I didn't see him," he said. "And I haven't seen

him in a long time."

"He's been in Kenya."

"How long?"

"A couple of years." I was beginning to lose him.

"He always liked the dry places."

"I'm sure that Sam will be calling here on Sunday looking for me." I changed the subject. This sometimes brought Taw back.

"It doesn't matter," he said. "He has no power to stop this."

"Stop what?"

Taw didn't answer me. In fact, he stopped talking altogether and just stared at the water going by. I had learned the best thing to do was to wait. Sometimes he came back and sometimes he didn't.

Half an hour passed. I sat next to him and looked at the water and wondered what he was seeing. *"Look at the white spaces."* In Taw's case, the white spaces were huge—much too large to understand.

"I have something for you," he said.

I looked up at him. He was staring at me, and I wondered how long he had been watching me as I looked at the water.

He stood up. "It's in my room."

I checked my watch and saw that it was exactly eleven o'clock. I wondered if he'd still be with me when he woke up from his nap. We walked slowly to the building and into his room. Inside was a small desk, a bed, and next to it a nightstand with a lamp on it. On the desk was a photo of me taken several years before and a photo of my mom and dad at the Hopi reservation in Arizona. They were smiling and waving out the window of an old abandoned pueblo. It was the only time we had been there.

"I brought some photos and letters from Dad," I said. "I was wondering if you could keep them for me until I get back." I held out the manila envelope.

He took it without looking inside and put it in the desk drawer. He then opened another drawer and pulled out a small cardboard box and handed it to me.

Inside was a Hopi kachina figurine, about five inches long, carved out of the root of a cottonwood tree. It was the smallest kachina I'd ever seen.

"The kachina are the spirits that helped us learn the art of surviving in this world," he said. "They are with us from December to July; after that they go back."

I held the figure in my hand and looked at it. "Did you make this?"

"No," he said, sitting down on the bed. "It has been in the family for a long time."

It looked very old, and I didn't want to lose it on my trip. "Maybe I should leave it here," I said.

"No, you keep it." He slipped his shoes off and lay down on the bed. "Kachinas know how to take care of themselves. They like to travel."

"Which kachina is this?" I asked.

But Taw didn't answer, because he had already fallen asleep.

I played chess with Peter while Taw slept, but my head wasn't into it. After beating me twice he asked if I wanted a rematch.

I looked at my watch. "Not today," I said, and stood up. "Taw should be up by now. I want to say good-bye, then catch my train."

I walked to Taw's room, but he wasn't there. He must have gone back to his chair by the creek. I went out back and looked, but he wasn't there, either. I asked a couple of people where he was, but no one seemed to know. I went back inside and found Peter.

"I can't seem to find my grandfather."

"He's not in his room or out back?"

I shook my head.

"Well, he can't be too far," Peter said.

We searched the home, then went back outside— still no sign of him. I began to worry that he had wandered away. If that happened there was no way that I could leave.

Peter found one of the nurses. "Have you seen Lansa?"

"I think he's in the basement," she said.

"The basement?" Both Peter and I were surprised. I didn't even know there was a basement. "What's he doing down there?"

She shrugged her shoulders. "A couple of hours ago, he and Frank and a few others said they were going down there to work on a project. Mary was with them, so I didn't think it was any big deal." Mary had been a volunteer at the home for years.

"He didn't take his nap?" I asked.

"I guess not," she said.

"I wonder what the old bird's up to," Peter asked.

I wondered, too.

Peter led me to a door and opened it. I hoped Taw was down there. I was running out of time. We heard voices as we walked down the stairs. The talking stopped as soon as we came around the corner. A group of people was standing near a workbench. Among them was Taw. I was very relieved to see him. In the air was the strong smell of enamel paint.

"What have you been doing down here?" Peter asked.

"A going-away present for Jake," Taw said happily. He turned around and picked up something behind him. When he turned back he was holding my bike helmet out to me proudly.

I couldn't believe it. They had painted the helmet with black-and-white stripes, like a zebra. I was too shocked to say anything. I couldn't wear a helmet painted like a zebra! And I wouldn't have time to get another one before I left for Kenya.

"And that's not all!" he said happily. "Bring it out, Joe!"

From behind the furnace, Joe wheeled my bike into the light. It was painted exactly like my helmet.

"That's something you don't see every day," Peter said.

He was right about that.

"What do you think?" Taw asked.

"I don't know what to say."

"We thought you'd like it," he said. "They paint airplanes like this in Africa so they won't scare the animals. We've seen it on television documentaries!"

So much for the secret. The entire home now knew that I was going to Africa, and Sam would know as soon as he called the home looking for me.

"I thought you were taking a nap," I said.

"I wasn't tired."

I looked at him and grinned. There was really nothing else I could do. "Thanks, Taw," I said, and hugged him.

I wheeled the bike up the stairs and outside. They had done a very professional job—each stripe was nearly perfect. I was embarrassed—so much for being inconspicuous in Kenya. Everyone gathered around the bike to admire it as I put the panniers back on. The paint was still wet—it wasn't going to be easy to keep it off my pants on the ride back to the train station.

I looked at my watch. "I better be going." I gave Taw another hug and swung on to my bike. "See you when I get back," I said, and started to pedal away. I looked back and saw the group waving to me. I waved back and hoped that my unusual bike didn't cause too many auto accidents on the way to the train station.

As I waited for the train I wrote Sam a note.

> Dear Sam,
>   By the time you get this letter, I will be well on my way to Kenya to see my father. I couldn't tell you because there is no way you would have let me go. I am sorry for the worry I've caused you.
>   Please don't delay your trip to Honduras on account of me. You won't be able to find me anyway. Don't worry about me! I know what I'm doing, and I'll be fine.
> Jake

PART II
Kenya

"Two nights ago I saw you walking in a big land. You were not alone, but I could not see who you were with."

Nine

On the airplane I studied my Swahili book. Most Kenyans speak three languages: their tribal tongue, English, and Swahili. Swahili spread from the east coast of Kenya to the interior during the slave trade. I read that even though Kenyans spoke English, they appreciated it when you tried to speak Swahili, which was the unofficial language of the country.

I had very little money and a bike painted like a zebra. Other than this, things were perfect because the airplane was on its final approach to the Kenyatta International Airport. I had arrived.

A blast of dry heat hit me as I stepped into the corridor leading to the terminal. Inside, I got into the short customs line. Having traveled internationally a couple of times with my mom, I knew what to expect.

"Passport," the uniformed custom official said.

I handed him my passport. He looked at the photo, then back to me, then back to the photo. He checked the visa.

"Tourist?" He was all business and not very friendly.

"Yes," I said.

"Your tickets."

I handed him my airline tickets. He scrutinized these very carefully.

"You have not booked a return flight?"

"No," I said.

"How long will you be here?"

"I'm not sure," I said.

"Your visa is good for three months."

"I know."

"You are young."

"I'm meeting my father," I said, and I was about to give him the bogus letter, when he handed my tickets and passport back and waved me to the baggage carousel. I felt very relieved.

I found my panniers and the cardboard box with my bike in it. With some difficulty, I pushed them over to the baggage line. The three people in front of me were moved through the baggage check very quickly.

"Passport." Another uniformed customs agent, about as friendly as the first one. He looked at my passport, then handed it back.

"What's in the box?"

"My bicycle."

He looked mildly surprised. "Open it."

I tore the cardboard away, and my bike helmet fell out and skidded across the floor. I heard laughter behind me and turned.

"You dropped something." A tourist with a big grin on his face held my helmet out to me.

I was very embarrassed. Why hadn't Taw taken his nap? I took the helmet and turned back. There were now two customs agents looking at my bike. They were laughing and speaking Swahili. So much for breezing through customs. They'd be talking about this for a week.

"What is the bicycle for?" The customs agent asked.

"For riding," I said.

"A bush bike?"

This got a big laugh from everyone except me. "Sort of," I said.

Another agent came over—obviously the man in charge. He looked at the bike, then at me, then at the other agents. He said something in Swahili and they stopped smiling.

"You are to follow him," one of the agents said.

This was not going the way I wanted. I was in trouble. I put the panniers on the back of the bike and pushed it behind the unsmiling man in charge. He led me to a small office and when we got inside he shut the door behind us.

"Passport and ticket," he said.

As he scrutinized them I nervously looked around the room. It was painted institutional green and there was nothing in it except a long table.

"Your business in Kenya."

"I'm here to see my father," I said with more confidence than I felt.

"And who is your father?"

"Dr. Robert Lansa," I said, emphasizing the "doctor," hoping that it would impress him. He didn't look impressed.

"Where is he?"

"He'll be here in a couple of days," I lied.

He stared at me, and I tried to stare back at him, but without much success.

"Where is he?" he repeated.

"He's in the bush," I said. "He's a field biologist for the Wildlife Research Institute."

"I see," he said. "Why isn't he here to meet you?"

"He had things to take care of in the field," I said. "I'm to wait for him at the hotel."

"Which hotel?"

I fumbled a slip of paper out of my pocket. The travel agent had given me the name of a reasonably priced hotel in Nairobi. I figured that I would need to spend a night there in order to rest after the long flight.

"The Mara," I said.

"I see." He stared at me again.

I felt sweat pouring down my neck, soaking my shirt. "He'll meet me at the hotel," I said.

"You said that."

"*They relish making you squirm with their squirts of power.*" I felt like a worm in a frying pan.

"What is in the bags?"

"Just my stuff."

"Open them and put the contents on the table."

I took everything out and spread it on the table.

"Now your pockets," he said.

I pulled out my pocket knife, wallet, matches, and the kachina figure.

"What is this?" he asked, picking up the kachina.

"It's called a kachina," I said. "From the Hopi Indian tribe of America."

"It looks like a doll," he said. "You are American Indian?"

"Half," I said. "My father's full-blooded Hopi."

"What is the doll for?"

"My grandfather wanted me to give it to my father."

Uninterested, he gave the kachina back to me and pointed to the packages of food. "And these?"

"Freeze-dried food," I said.

He nodded and took my knife and opened a package of beef Stroganoff. "This is food?"

"You add boiling water."

He put his finger in the open package and tasted it. "You cannot bring food into Kenya," he said.

Great, I thought, people are starving to death, but you can't bring food into Kenya.

"One of the reasons I brought the food was so I wouldn't be taking food from those who need it," I said.

Ignoring my noble reasoning, he took another taste. "And these others?"

"Food," I said.

"Food is not allowed to be brought in," he repeated.

I was going to object again, but I thought better of it.

He picked up all the food packages and put them to the side, then proceeded to look through the rest of my gear. When he was finished he said, "You may put your things back, but not the food." He stared at me for a moment, getting in one final squirt, then said, "You may go."

He watched while I hurriedly loaded the panniers. I looked at him again before I left.

"I hope you enjoy your visit to Kenya," he said.

"I hope so, too," I said, and left the room pushing my bike.

I wheeled the bike through the airport amid laughter and grins, but I was now too relieved to be embarrassed. They had taken the food, but I had made it through. Getting into Kenya was the last official obstacle—all I had to do now was find my father.

On the way out I stopped at the currency booth and exchanged my hundred and fifty dollars for a little over a thousand shillings.

When I got outside I was accosted by several men offering me rides to the city in their taxis. My original plan was to ride my bike into the city, but the long flight and hassle in customs changed that. All I wanted to do was get to the hotel and sleep. I agreed on a price with one of the cabbies. We figured out a way to tie the bike on the back and left the airport.

The road to Nairobi was jammed with cars, trucks, buses, and motorcycles. I sat in the back looking out the window as the cab driver maneuvered his car expertly through the snarl of traffic. It wasn't much different from being on a road in the U.S., except there were more Land Rovers and Toyota Land Cruisers, and the cars were older. Outside of the city, we passed an area that was covered with tin-roofed shanties and tents for as far as I could see. I asked the driver what it was.

"Refugees," he said. "They come here because of the drought, but there is nothing for them here."

A large group of children sat on the side of the road staring blankly at the passing cars. They were very thin and their clothes were little more than rags. I'd seen famine victims on television, but it was nothing like seeing them in person. Even from the taxi I could see their suffering.

The traffic got worse as we entered the city. At one point my driver jumped out of the car and started yelling at the driver in front of him. It didn't make any sense because the driver in front was bumper to bumper with the car in front of him, and so on down the line. After he pushed the other driver around for a few moments he got back into the car as if nothing had happened.

"It is the same every day," he said.

I hadn't set foot in the city, and already I wanted to leave. The sidewalks were full of people. It looked like New York, except the people weren't walking. They were simply standing on the sidewalks talking to each other and looking at the traffic.

"What are all these people doing?" The driver didn't seem to understand. I tried again. "Why are they just standing around?"

"Nothing else to do," he said.

"What about work?"

He laughed. "There are no jobs in Nairobi."

A few moments later we pulled up in front of the hotel. He untied my bike; I paid him, then walked inside.

The hotel clerk behind the front desk stared at my bike. I ignored his reaction and told him that I wanted a room for the night.

He took my money and handed me a key. "Your room is on the second floor," he said, pointing to the left. "The stairs are over there."

"Thanks," I said.

I pushed my bike through the lobby. At one time the hotel had probably been very nice, but it was obvious that nothing had been done to it in a long time. The wallpaper was yellow with age, and the ceiling was missing plaster in spots. Several worn chairs and sofas were scattered in front of an old black-and-white television set. The volume was on loud and the fuzzy picture flickered.

I bounced my bike up the stairs to the second floor and found my room. There wasn't much to it—an old double bed, a small desk, a window, and a bathroom. It wasn't air-conditioned, but I didn't care. I leaned my bike against the wall, stripped off my clothes, and got into the shower. There was hardly any pressure, and the water smelled like sulfur, but it felt like a cool spring to me. When I finished, I lay down on the bed and immediately fell asleep.

The room was dark when I woke up, and for a moment, I didn't know where I was. I lay there getting my bearings and wondered how long I'd slept. I sat up and turned on the lamp next to the bed. My bike was leaning against the opposite wall. The room was stiflingly hot. I got out of bed and with some effort managed to get the window open. A cool breeze blew in, along with the sound of cars and people's voices. The street below was even more crowded than it had been during the day.

When I went down to the lobby a different clerk stood behind the counter reading a newspaper.

"Excuse me," I said.

He put the paper down and seemed surprised that the hotel had a guest.

"Yes," he said. "May I help you?"

"I'm looking for canned food."

"Canned?"

"Yeah. Like soup and meat—in cans."

He looked confused. The afternoon clerk seemed to have a better understanding of English.

"Food," I said. "In cans."

"I understand food," he said.

"Preserved food—in cans."

He thought about it another moment. "Do you mean tinned food?"

"Right," I said.

"We have no tinned food here," he said.

"I know," I said. "Where's the nearest grocery store?"

"For tinned food?"

"Yes."

"Two miles away, on this street. To the left."

"*Asante*," I said, which is Swahili for "thank you."

I went back up to my room and got my bike. As I was crossing the lobby with it, the clerk stopped me.

"Where are you going?" he asked.

"To get tinned food," I said.

"No, no, no," he said. "You must not go out now. It is not safe now."

"But I'm leaving town in the morning. What time does the store open?"

"At eight."

"Too late," I said. "I'll be leaving at sunrise, and I need to take food with me."

"It is not safe."

"I'll be all right."

He shrugged his shoulders and went back to his newspaper.

I rode down the street passing cinemas, restaurants, hotels, and nightclubs. It was surprisingly cool, and I wished that I had brought my jacket. People stared at my bike and pointed at me as I rode by. I hoped the store had paint—I didn't need all this attention. Asante, Taw.

When I got to the store I chained my bike to a

post and locked it. The store was small and there was more space on the shelves than items.

I collected a few cans of soup, tuna, sardines, and meat, and a couple of loaves of bread, then looked around for paint, but I didn't find any.

I took the cans up to the counter and the clerk added it up. "That will be 249 shillings," he said.

"What?" That was about thirty-five dollars—a quarter of my money and I only had ten cans of food. "Why so expensive?"

He shrugged his shoulders. I had brought four hundred shillings with me, figuring that it was more than enough for groceries, paint, and perhaps a meal in a restaurant on the way back to the hotel. I guess food gets expensive when it's scarce. I paid him and walked out of the store with my bag of gold.

When I got outside, I stared in disbelief at the post my bike had been locked to. The chain had been cut in two like a piece of twine and my bike was gone. I hadn't been in the store more than ten minutes.

I dropped the groceries and ran into the middle of the street just in time to see three people disappear around the corner about a block away. One of them was riding my bike as the other two ran alongside. I yelled and started to run after them. When I got to the corner I saw they had dropped my helmet. Barely breaking stride, I scooped it up and continued to pursue them. I yelled again and saw them turn another corner. I ran up to the corner and stopped. They had gone down a dark narrow street.

This is stupid, Jake! But I didn't have any choice—my bike was my transportation to my father's camp. I walked down the street very slowly. What was

71

I going to do if I found them? I put my helmet on and tightened the strap around my chin.

Me: *I'm afraid there's been a mistake—that's my bike you have there.*
Thieves: *Oh really? We're sorry—we didn't know. Here, take it back.*

I told myself to walk to the hotel and call the police, but they'd ask questions that I didn't have good answers to, like "Where's your father?" and "How old are you?"

About halfway down the street I stopped. My courage got lost somewhere in the dark. There had to be another way to my father's camp.

I heard something behind me, and before I could turn, I got hit in the back. The air in my lungs rushed out as I slammed into the ground. Another hit—not as bad as the first, but it left a searing pain in my shoulder. I curled up into a ball and covered my face. The blows came from all directions now. I heard angry voices and grunts, then I passed out.

It was still dark when I opened my eyes. Every inch of my body ached and I was very cold. I sat up slowly. The buildings spun around my head; I felt nauseous and thought I was going to black out again, but instead, I threw up all over my lap. That's when I realized that my pants were gone. I sat there for a long time thinking about what this meant. They had taken my pants, shirt, shoes, and my bike. I felt my head. My helmet was gone. I was two miles from the hotel and I had barf on my bare legs. They hadn't taken my underwear. I felt around my neck—the amulet was still there. They must have missed it in the dark. I was glad about that.

A cold wind blew down the street. How could it be so cold at night and so hot during the day? *"Nairobi is at five thousand feet; when the sun sets it gets very cold."* I had to get back to the hotel. I wondered if my legs were broken. It was hard to tell where one hurt stopped and another started. I moved my legs one at a time. In spite of the pain, they seemed to work. Very, very slowly I got to my feet, using a wall to steady myself. The light of the street was only half a block away. I took a step and felt my knees buckle and caught myself on the wall. *"Survival is more important than getting there."* I had my whole life to get to the hotel and I thought, At the rate I'm going, it might just take that long.

It took ten minutes for me to reach the end of the street. By then, my head had cleared a little, and I had regained some of my strength.

Twenty minutes later I passed the store, which was now closed. My canned food was long gone.

People stared at me as I walked by. No one said anything, and no one offered to help.

It took me two hours to reach the hotel. The clerk was still on duty. I went up to the desk and asked for the key to my room.

"What happened?"

"Just give me my key," I said. I didn't want to get into it with him.

He gave me the key. "Your bike?" he asked.

"It's gone."

I didn't give him a chance to ask about my

clothes. I just walked away and climbed the stairs to my room.

I went into the bathroom and surveyed the damage in the mirror. An ugly bruise was forming on my shoulder, and I was sure there were more bruises on my back. Other than this, I seemed to be okay physically. My mental condition was another story. I felt disoriented—it was like everything that had happened since I left New York had not actually occurred. Had my bike really been painted like a zebra? Had it been stolen, along with my clothes? Was I really in Africa?

I slipped on another pair of jeans and a T-shirt and flopped down on the bed. I had no idea what I was going to do. I couldn't sleep. I lay there for a long time and stared at the cracks in the ceiling.

There was knock on the door. Painfully, I got up from the bed and opened it. An African in a starched khaki uniform stood there.

"Hello," he said. "I'm a police officer. I hear there's been a problem."

The hotel clerk must have called him. "It's really no big deal," I said.

He smiled and looked at a small notebook. "The clerk says that you came into the hotel in your underwear and that your bike was stolen."

"That's right," I said. "But it's really no big deal."

"An attack on a tourist in Kenya is always a big deal," he said. "You are Jacob Lansa?"

I nodded.

"I must make a report," he said. "May I come in?"

"Sure." I let him in.

I told him what I was doing in Kenya and what had happened. And I prayed that he wouldn't put me

74

into protective custody or something until my father showed up.

"Can you describe them?"

"No," I said. "I never saw them up close. What are the chances of getting my bike back?"

He shook his head. "We will look, but you will probably not see it again. I'm afraid that tourists are not safe these days." He looked at his notebook for a moment. "Your father will be here tomorrow?"

"Yes." Here it comes, I thought. *Perhaps you should come with me until your father arrives.*

"Until then, I advise you not to go out," he said. "If you need anything else you can reach me at this number." He handed me a card and turned to go, then stopped. "Please do not judge us by this incident. Kenya is a beautiful country, but we are having some problems now. Your bicycle and clothes will be sold for food. Many have no choice other than to steal. I am sorry."

"It's all right," I said. "I don't blame you or your country."

He smiled and walked out of my room.

I was glad to see that not all Kenyan officials had the need to squirt people with their power.

Ten

I slept through the morning despite the heat, which by noon had turned the room into an oven. I was being baked alive, and I understood why everyone stood outside on the street—it was better than dying indoors.

I sat up slowly, acutely aware of every muscle in my body, because all of them were screaming at me not to move. My right shoulder was very tender. Every time I moved it, a searing pain shot all the way through to my fingertips. My back was also very sore from whatever they had hit me with. I got to my feet. The room swerved a little, but I was feeling much steadier than I had the night before. I guessed I'd live. I took a shower and continued to stand under the spigot long after the warm water ran out. After I dried off and dressed I realized that I was famished. The last time I'd eaten was on the airplane and I'd lost most of that meal.

I went downstairs and asked for directions to the nearest restaurant. The clerk directed me to a good one a couple of blocks away. The meal helped to lift my spirits somewhat. Afterward, I walked around for a while thinking about my options. I decided to call the institute and see if they had heard from my father. I found a pay phone and dropped a coin into it.

"Wildlife Research Institute." It was the same woman I had talked to before.

"This is Jacob Lansa."

"How are you?"

I ached all over; my bike, clothes, and part of my money were stolen. "Good," I said, trying to sound cheerful. "Have you heard from my father?"

"In a roundabout way," she said. "He sent a note to us, but I'm not sure that he has gotten any of our messages."

"What did the note say?"

"It said that he was staying in the bush," she said.

"Doesn't he know that the institute is closed down?" I asked.

"I'm sure he does," she said, "but he doesn't want to leave his elephants. He says that he's going to stay out there until we reopen."

"When will that be?"

"I'm not sure," she said. "I'm the last person here, and I'm leaving tonight. You were lucky to catch me. The phone is supposed to be disconnected this afternoon."

"Did he mention where he was?"

"Not specifically," she said.

"Doesn't he have a radio?"

"Yes, but it has a very short range, and we haven't been able to reach him on it."

"What does all of this mean?"

"I guess it means that he is going to stay out there until he decides to come in."

"Your dad's pretty damn stubborn." I had been hoping that he might have already come in, that he might answer the phone. . . .

Me: Hi, Dad.

Dad: Jacob! I just talked to Sam. He had a crazy story about
    you being in Kenya.
Me: I'm here, Dad.
Dad: No kidding. . . . That's great!

"Well, thanks," I said.

"I wouldn't worry about him," she said sympathetically. "He knows how to take care of himself."

"Yeah," I said. "I guess you're right."

My choices were to fly back to New York, walk to my father's camp, or try to get another bike and ride there. I decided that a bike was my best option.

But I soon found that Nairobi was not the best place in the world to buy a bike. Good bikes were hard to find and expensive. I found a shop that had a couple of mountain bikes but they wanted the equivalent of three hundred dollars for them, and they weren't quality bikes. Another shop had used bikes, but I doubted any of them would hold up where I was going. It was very discouraging.

I ended up in a bazaar near the center of the city because one of the shop owners told me that bikes were sometimes sold there. It was jammed with tourists. If tourism was down, I would have hated to see it when it was up. The bazaar had everything imaginable for sale. Stone and wooden carvings, native jewelry, beautiful cloth, food, and animal skins. I took a close look at the skins. Zebra, impala, bush buck, and even giraffe skins hung on long sturdy poles.

" 'Scuse me, 'scuse me."

A young boy came up to me. He couldn't have been more than seven years old.

"Jambo *sana*," he said, which is Swahili for "very good morning," "very good evening," "hello"—all rolled into one.

"*Habari?*" I replied, which literally means, "what's your news?"

"*Mazuri*," he said. Mazuri meant "good," and in Swahili you always said mazuri, even if your news wasn't good.

"Do you like the skins?" he asked in pretty good English.

"I like them better on the animals," I said.

"Do you like ivory?"

"What do you mean?" There was a ban on ivory—it was illegal to sell or possess "white gold."

He reached into his pocket and pulled out a small ivory carving. "Do you like this?"

It was carved in the shape of an antelope, and I had to admit that it was very nice. "No," I said. "I don't like it. And it's not legal to sell ivory in Kenya."

He must have understood what I said, because he quickly put the carving back in his pocket. "Do you want to buy a skin?"

"No I don't," I said. "I'm looking for bikes."

"Bikes?"

"A bicycle."

"Yes, yes," he said excitedly. "I know where bicycles are. I show you bicycles."

I followed him through the narrow rows of the bazaar lined with vendors on both sides. It was like a maze, and I began to wonder if I'd be able to find my way out. We seemed to be leaving the tourist area of the bazaar and entering a public market section. People argued loudly over the price of fruit and meat.

Crates with live chickens were stacked all over the place, and small herds of goats were held behind rickety fences. For a starving country there was a lot of food standing around. The air was filled with flies and the smell of rotting fruit and meat. I saw no tourists in this section of the bazaar; it was as if the odor had set up an invisible barrier.

"Wait a second," I yelled to the boy leading me. He stopped and came back. "Where is this place?"

"Not far," he said. "Come." He moved off again.

I didn't follow him right away. I was beginning to get a bad feeling about the situation. I felt vulnerable—especially after the night before.

"Come!" he yelled.

Reluctantly, I continued to follow. He led me past the food stands and into a large warehouse. Inside were more vendors. I swatted at the flies buzzing around my face.

"Come," he said. "Over here. Bicycles!"

I followed him around a corner and he was right—there were bicycles. Several bicycles, as a matter of fact, and right in the middle of them was a mountain bike painted like a zebra with my helmet hanging on the handlebars.

"I told you," he said.

"Asante," I said, not looking at him because I couldn't take my eyes off my bike.

"I told you," he repeated and tugged on my shirt sleeve.

I looked at him and saw that he had his hand out. I gave him some change.

"Asante," I said again, and he ran off into the crowd.

I walked over to my bike. There were a few new scratches here and there, but other than that it looked in good shape.

"Hello!"

I turned to see a small man who looked East Indian standing behind me. He was short and had not shaved for several days—and by the stale smell coming from him, I doubted that he had bathed recently either.

"Do you like the bicycle?" he asked.

"Yeah," I said.

"Good, good, good! Do you want to buy it?"

"It's my bike," I said quietly.

"Yes, yes, yes," he said. "A good bike, and I will make you a good price on the good bike."

"You don't understand," I said. "This is *my* bike!"

"Yes," he said. "I will sell it to you for three hundred and fifty American dollars. A good price!"

"I'm not going to buy it! It's my bike. It was stolen from me last night!"

"Stolen?" He feigned surprise.

"Right."

"Last night?"

"Right."

"No, no, no," he said. "I have this bicycle for many weeks."

"That's a lie," I said.

"But I have the bike for three, no, four weeks," he said.

"No way!"

"I will sell it to you for three hundred!" he said.

I thought about going to the police, but if I did, I was sure that my bike would be gone when I got back.

"I don't have that much money," I said. "And I'm not going to buy it, because it belongs to me."

"How much will you pay?" he asked.

I didn't want to pay anything, but giving him some money might be the easiest way to get the bike back.

"I can give you fifty dollars," I said, holding out a wad of shillings.

He laughed. "Fifty dollars? The bicycle is worth much more than that. My final offer is two hundred and fifty."

"I don't have that much," I said.

"Then perhaps I can interest you in another bicycle."

"No," I said, and got on the bike.

"What are you doing?" he asked angrily.

We glared at each other for several moments, then his eyes shifted to something behind me and he smiled. I turned and looked. Behind the long row of bikes stood three young Africans. They were also smiling. One of them wore my jeans, another wore my shirt, and the third held my knife, with the blade open—flipping it menacingly from one hand to the other.

"Get off the bicycle," the man said.

I swung off the bike very slowly, not letting go of the handlebars and not taking my eyes off the three thieves.

"The police know you took the bike," I said. "I made a report."

The news didn't seem to disturb them.

We were at the end of a row. The only other person in sight was an old woman across the way selling pots and pans. She was sitting in a chair reading a newspaper, unaware that we were even there.

I took a deep breath and kicked the bike nearest to me, which knocked over the others. At the same time I started forward, pushing my bike. The man grabbed my arm. I jerked away and swung, hitting him in the chest. He fell backward onto a table filled with wooden carvings. When I got to the aisle I began to run with my bike. I looked back and saw the three men trying to scramble over the row of toppled bikes.

When I had enough momentum, I swung on and started to pedal. I rode furiously through the warehouse and out into the market. Behind me I heard angry shouts. I turned my head and saw the three thieves running after me. It was hard to maneuver down the narrow rows. They were gaining. Alerted by the shouts, another vendor came out of his booth and tried to grab me as I rode by. I swerved and kicked out at the same time, sending him flying backward.

My only chance of escape was to get into the open, but I had no idea how to get out of the market. I rode down one aisle, turned, and rode down another aisle, and then I saw the vendor I had kicked. I was riding in a circle! There had to be a way out of this maze. The thieves were no longer behind me and I thought that I had lost them, then I turned another corner and saw them again—only this time they were in front of me! I slammed on the brakes and skidded to a stop, turned, and pedaled in the opposite direction. I turned again, and about halfway down the aisle I realized that I had entered a dead end. I stopped and looked back. The thieves were at the end of the aisle. They began to move in my direction. I looked around, panicked. All of the vendors stood by their booths looking at me. It had gotten very quiet. I pedaled to the booth at the end of the row and swung off my bike. The back wall of the booth was made of cloth. I shoved the cloth to the side and pushed my bike through to the other side. Behind were bushes and trees. The back of the booth was on the edge of a very steep hillside.

I didn't hesitate. I jumped on my bike and went over the edge. The hillside was not only steep, it was also long. I gently applied the brakes in order to slow down, but my bike began to skid out from under me. I released the brakes and got it back in line, but this increased the speed. I didn't dare look behind for fear of hitting something in front of me. Even if they were after me, there was no way they would catch up unless I ran into a tree—in which case I would probably break my neck and then what difference would it make if they caught me? I applied the brakes, went into a skid, let the brakes off, and gathered speed—all the way down the hillside. I finally got to the bottom of the hill and stopped.

I was drenched in sweat and breathing hard. I looked back up the hill and didn't see anyone after me. I felt exhilarated and victorious. I let out a whoop of joy. I was going to get my things and get out of Nairobi as fast as I could pedal.

Eleven

On the way out of town I rode by the refugee camp. The view from my bike was much worse than it had been from the cab. The people looked like walking skeletons. Flies crawled on their faces, and they were either too weak to brush them away or they were so used to them that they didn't care. Most of the refugees were from Somalia and Ethiopia, where the effects of the drought were worse then they were in Kenya. The stench of the camp burned my nostrils.

I had purchased more food and heard the cans clanking together in the panniers as I rode. I felt guilty and thought about stopping and tossing the cans to them. But would it do any good? How long would it last if it were distributed in the camp? A day? Two days? Then what?

I rode on by with my food and my guilt.

The heat shimmered over the Rift Valley in waves. It was unbelievably hot.

About twenty miles outside of Nairobi, the land began to open up. I passed farms and ranches. Acacia trees dotted the arid landscape. If it hadn't been for the zebras and impalas standing in the fields, I would have sworn I was back in the States, riding my bike along a country road on a very hot August day.

The road was paved and narrow and full of potholes. Aside from an occasional bus or Land Rover, there was no traffic.

Up ahead I saw several large dark birds surrounding a lump in the road. They hopped away awkwardly as I approached. I stopped for a moment next to the lump and saw that it was a road-killed hyena, bloating in the heat. I held my breath and swatted at the swarm of flies buzzing around the carcass. The hyena's eyes were gone, and white maggots squirmed around the empty sockets. The dark birds were vultures—too gorged with food to fly away. They stood ten feet off the road, waiting for me to leave so they could continue their feast.

I pedaled down the road and did not let my breath out until I was well past the stink of the hyena.

A few miles later I passed three young Masai, about my age, walking along the road toward Nairobi. I wanted to stop and tell them that there was nothing in the city for them, but what would be the point? I simply waved, and one of them waved back. Each carried a long spear, and they wore the traditional red Masai *shuka*, which look like the togas that the ancient Romans wore. Their hair was braided and caked with red clay. They must have been young warriors, called *morans*.

My father had told me that the Masai are one of the few tribes that have maintained much of their culture. They are nomads, and their wealth is based on the number of cattle and goats they keep. The cows and nannies are milked and bled and, only on special occasions, eaten.

The Masai live in small family communities called

kraals. The kraals are encircled by a high wall of dried thorn bushes to keep predators and enemies out. Inside the kraal are small huts made of sticks and plastered with cow dung.

The Masai follow the grass with their herds. I wondered how they were doing in the drought. So far I hadn't seen a single blade of green grass.

As I rode along I smelled the sweet scent of heat, dust, and smoke. The only thing I heard was my breathing and my thoughts.

I passed a small herd of wildebeests. When they saw me they ran a few hundred yards, stopped, and looked back. I knew that I would see a lot more of them. *"When the wildebeests are migrating, you'll see tens of thousands of them in one group making their way across the savanna."* I stopped for a drink of water, finishing off my first bottle. I was still thirsty, and I only had one bottle left. Water could be a problem between towns.

My plan was to camp along the side of the road and then reach the small town of Suswa the following morning to replenish my water supply. Then on to Narok, Ewaso Ngiro, Barkitabu, and Morijo. Outside Narok, the road wasn't paved, and this would slow me down. I'd have to keep my eyes open for sources of water. During the survival course in Arizona I got high marks in finding water. *"If you can find water on a regular basis, you've solved fifty percent of your problems."* The other problems were shelter and food. If it didn't take too long to get to my father's camp I would have plenty of food. If I ran out I could always buy food in the towns—although I had very little money left. I didn't think shelter was going to be a problem. During the day

I'd keep my helmet on to protect me from the sun, and at night I'd start a fire and wrap myself up in my sleeping bag.

At about seven in the evening I found a good spot to camp, near a large baobab tree. Baobabs are squat trees with trunks as wide as thirty feet in diameter. They look as though they have been uprooted and put back in the ground upside down.

As the sun set, the temperature dropped dramatically. It wasn't as cool as the highlands of Nairobi, but it was still a relief from the heat of the day. I gathered wood and built a small fire.

I leaned against the trunk of the tree and swatted at flies. I was exhausted and sore, and I didn't know if this was from the beating or if I was just out of shape. I'd made pretty good time, but the ride had been mostly downhill. I wondered what it would be like once I left the paved road.

I took the water bottle out of the pannier and thought about squirting some into my mouth, then put it back without opening it. I'd need the water tomorrow—the soup would be enough fluid for now.

When the soup was ready I made myself eat it very slowly. By the time I finished, it was dark. A light breeze began to buffet the flames of the fire. I unrolled my sleeping bag, lay on top of it, and fell into an exhausted sleep.

The next morning I awoke just as the sun was rising. I packed my things and left the camp without eating because I wanted to take advantage of the relatively cool morning.

I reached Suswa by midmorning and only stayed

there long enough to replenish my water and buy a couple of loaves of bread.

I pedaled steadily throughout the day. The farther west I went, the more animals I saw. Small groups of Thompson's gazelles, giraffes, bush bucks, topi, zebras, and impalas grazed by the roadside. During the hottest part of the day the animals stood in the scant shade of the acacia trees.

That night I camped by the roadside again. I was too tired to start a fire. The soup was warm anyway from sitting in the pannier all day.

The next afternoon I filled my water bottles in the small town of Seyabei. Outside of town I stopped on a bridge and got out my map. The river under the bridge was called the Siyiapel. It flowed into the Ewaso Ngiro, which was the river that ran along the base of the Nguruman Escarpment, where my father's camp was located.

My original plan was to keep heading west past Narok and then take the dirt road south to Morijo and from there head east over the Lebetero Hills. It was a roundabout way to my father's camp, but at least I'd be near the roads and civilization in case something happened. On the other hand, if I left the road now and followed the river I'd save a lot of time. Not only that, but I would have a source of drinking water along the way.

I looked at the water below the bridge. The banks of the river were very steep. The only way down to the water were narrow paths made by animals. A green scum grew on the surface and there was hardly any flow. The water would have to be purified. I had tablets to remove the bacteria.

I stared at the map and tried to imagine what it would be like traveling along the river. It was at least seventy miles to my father's camp, and there were no towns or settlements along the route.

It was getting late and I was too tired to make a rational decision, so I decided not to decide. I made camp, ate a can of food, swatted at flies, and when it got dark, I fell asleep.

The next morning I opened my eyes just as the sun was rising, and I lay there breathing the cool morning air. I took a deep breath, closed my eyes, and listened. I heard birds chattering and the light breeze blowing through the trees.

The sounds reminded me of a camping trip with my father when I was eight years old. One night the wind began to really blow, and not far away from us a coyote started yapping. I was frightened. *There's nothing to be afraid of. The wind and coyote belong here. Just listen to them. Imagine that you're a coyote standing on a ridge, howling into the wind.* I learned to listen on that trip and not to be afraid of what I heard.

I slowly opened my eyes. Weaver birds were tending their delicate teardrop-shaped nests. The nests hung from the branches like Christmas tree ornaments.

I walked up to the road and looked west, then turned and looked south along the river. I decided that it was time to venture into the real Africa.

I got out my compass and plotted a course on the map. I packed my panniers, took a long drink of water, and began following the river.

Throughout the day I followed a crude trail along the river. The ride was difficult; I stopped every ten miles, drank water, reset the odometer on my bike, and started off again. The water level in the river dropped drastically. In some places there was no water at all—just a wide expanse of dried cracked mud.

Late that afternoon, about halfway through my third ten miles, a warthog and her three babies blasted out of some bushes right in front of me. I skidded to a stop and watched them run away as my heart pounded in my chest. I stayed there until my pulse returned to normal.

A couple of miles later it suddenly became very difficult to pedal. I stopped and saw that my rear tire had gone flat. By the time I got it changed it would be time to make camp. Twenty-eight miles wasn't too bad for my first day off the road. If I kept up that pace I would be at the Nguruman Escarpment in three days—way ahead of schedule.

I took the tire off and saw that I had run over a thorn. I patched it and began to fill it with the hand pump. It was a long, sweaty job. When the tire was half inflated I paused for breath, then froze.

I don't know why, but I knew that something was behind me. The hair on the back of my neck stood on end. It's your imagination, Jake—now that you're really in the bush, your mind is playing tricks on you. Very, very slowly I turned my head.

Fifty feet away, lying in a crouched position, was a male lion. His battle-scarred face was surrounded by a dark bushy mane. His black-tipped tail flicked from side to side. So much for my imagination! My mouth felt like it was stuffed with an old sock. A feeling of dread spread through my body. My mind raced, but I remained perfectly still.

I'd been around lions in the zoo, but this was entirely different. *"The only thing you can do if you are face-fo-face with a lion is to stay still."* The zookeeper's theory was not to panic. Easy thing to say.

The lion's golden eyes drilled into me. If he attacked, I'd be torn to shreds. In my imagination I heard my bones snapping as the lion ate me. When he finished, the jackals and vultures would pick my bones clean and spread them along the river. Then the porcupines and rodents would gnaw on my bones until they were gone. After I was digested by the various animals I would become part of the African ecosystem forever. I didn't want to stay in Africa quite that long.

If I ran, he'd be on me faster than I could blink. I could barely breathe and the flies were driving me crazy.

The lion stood up. Here it comes! *Snap! Snap! Snap!* He yawned, and I saw his huge yellowed canine teeth. He shot squirts of pee out behind him, then scraped dirt over the piss with his hind paws and lay back down. I knew how a mouse felt when cornered by a domestic cat.

My legs began to go to sleep. I wouldn't be able to hold my position much longer. His tail began to flick back and forth again. The sun was going down. I had to do something.

The only weapon I had was the tire pump, which was still attached to the stem of the tire. I tightened my grip on the pump, took several deep breaths, and counted silently. One, two, three. . . . As soon as I moved he started toward me. Using the pump's rubber hose as a sling, I hurled the tire at him. The tire bounced off his forehead. He roared at the impact. All four paws came off the ground, and before he came back down he had twisted his body in the other direction. He hit the ground running and disappeared into the bush.

I stared at the space he had occupied seconds before. I wondered if it had actually happened. But it must have, because the tire and the pump were twenty feet away. I stood up. My legs were shaking badly, and I had to swallow several times to keep bile from coming up. I walked over to the tire and saw the spot where he had scraped dirt over his piss. It had happened.

The pump was still attached to the tire and it didn't look damaged. I carried it back to my bike and sat down.

Numbly, I gathered wood for a fire. There was plenty of it around, and it was as dry as tissue paper. I piled the wood up and dropped a match on it. In a second I had a bonfire going. I hoped it would keep the animals away.

I finished pumping the tire up and attached it to the bike frame, then gathered enough wood to keep the fire going through the night.

The sun began to set, casting long shadows over the ground.

I put more wood on the fire. I wasn't hungry, but I knew I had to eat. I opened a can of stew and put it near the fire to heat it.

I thought about Nebraska. Right now I would be in the bedroom with my cousin Myron.

"Around midnight we sneak out," he'd be saying.

"A buddy of mine has a car. We take baseball bats and we drive the roads and smash mailboxes. It's a blast!"

I could go back to Nairobi and catch a plane for New York. I could go back to the road and follow it to my father's camp. Or I could continue to follow the river and take my chances.

I thought about the lion and tried to apply the careful scientific logic that my parents had taught me. The lion was in good flesh and didn't look as though he had missed too many meals. He was probably just wandering around when he saw me. Maybe he heard the tire pump and came over to investigate the sound. If he'd been hungry he would have dashed in and killed me before I even knew he was there. At one point he even yawned. Perhaps, if I had waited long enough, he might have gotten bored and wandered away. There was plenty of game around, and lions rarely attack people.

I forced myself to eat half the can of stew, then set it aside. I sat so close to the fire I was sweating. Whatever I decided to do, I wouldn't be able to do it until morning. I unrolled my sleeping bag and lay on it with my back to the fire. I heard a hyena laughing in the distance and wondered if it was laughing at me. I felt very lonely.

Twelve

Throughout the night, every time I closed my eyes I saw the lion staring at me. I knew every scar and whisker on his face. It was like he had crawled inside me and was now crouched in my brain. I checked my watch every five minutes and I put wood on the fire at least a dozen times. Finally, the sun came up.

I cleaned the campsite, put the fire out, and packed my bags. I scooped the rest of the stew into my mouth, took a drink of water, swung onto my bike, and continued to follow the river south. I told myself that I was past the point of no return. My only alternative was to push farther into the bush.

Like a hamster in an exercise wheel, I put myself into a bicycle trance—pedaling on and on and on. In the far distance I saw large columns of smoke—no doubt from brush fires. In the early afternoon I saw a pride of lions across the river. I started to panic and look for a place to hide. I forced myself to stop and look across the river. Lounging under the shade of an acacia tree were a male, three females, and several cubs. They saw me but continued to groom themselves—they seemed not at all interested in the young man with the zebra-painted bike. I watched for a while, took a drink of water, then continued on my way.

About an hour later I saw my first group of elephants. They were on the other side of the riverbed drinking from a pool of stagnant water.

It was time for the hamster to get off the wheel for a little rest. I ate a piece of bread as I watched the elephants. They dug into the mud with their feet and trunks to get to fresher water. When they finished drinking they rolled in the wallows, coating themselves with a layer of mud. The coating helped protect them from the sun and insects. I thought about my father and wondered if he was watching elephants.

"Depending on the size of the elephant, it can lose thousands of pounds during a drought. . . ."

The six elephants were very thin, and I thought again of the people in the refugee camp. How long could they all survive without food?

I got back on my bicycle.

I came around a bend in the river and ran into a large group of cattle. I stopped and saw that three young Masai boys were guarding the herd. We looked at each other from about thirty feet away. I smiled, but they were suspicious and didn't return my smile.

"Jambo!" I said.

They talked excitedly to each other, then one of them approached me, while another one ran off.

"Jambo," I said again, wondering if they spoke Swahili.

"Habari?"

"Mazuri," I said, happy that we were at least able to say hello to each other.

"American?"

"Yes," I said, surprised he spoke English. He came closer and looked at my bike.

"Mountain bike," I said, gesturing toward the bike.

He nodded. "Very nice," he said. "You come!" He started to walk away. I hesitated. He turned back and smiled. "Come!"

I got off my bike and pushed it behind him. He led me over the top of a hill. On the other side was a Masai kraal. Inside the thorn-bush fence were five huts.

"Come!"

I followed him down the hill. Several Masai came out of the kraal to greet me. I had no idea what they were saying but they seemed very pleased to see me. They crowded around my bicycle and ran their hands over it. An old man with short-cropped white hair came out of the kraal, and the group parted to let him through. He looked at the bike, then at me. He smiled broadly—there wasn't a tooth in his mouth. He put his hand on the top of my head and said something I didn't understand.

"You can come inside," the boy said.

I was herded into the kraal. I explained to the boy what I was doing out there. He seemed to understand and translated what I said to the group. It was obvious that they were suffering in the drought, but they looked healthier than the people in the refugee camp.

The old man said something to me.

"You can stay here," the boy said.

I looked at my watch. It was wonderful to be with people again—especially friendly people, but I could still get in another ten miles before sunset.

"Tell him thank you," I said. "But I must be going."

The boy translated, and the old man looked very

disappointed. One of the women led me over to a crude well and offered me water. I thanked her and filled my empty bottle.

"I have to go," I told the boy.

"Yes," he said.

I pushed my bike out of the kraal and got on it. As I rode away the children followed, laughing and talking. When I got to the top of the hill they stopped and waved.

I felt a pang of regret as I rode farther south and wished that I had stayed with the Masai for a while.

I set up camp near the river. After I ate I took my map out and marked down my progress. At the rate I was going I would be at the Nguruman Escarpment in a couple of days. I poured the water the Masai had given me into a pot and put it on the fire to boil. After it was bubbling for a while, I dropped in a couple of purification tablets and took it off the fire.

I looked down at the river and saw a pair of otters wrestling with each other. On the other side of the river, a saddlebill stork walked along the shore looking for food. The stork's massive beak was red and black, with a yellow saddle across the base. Every once in a while it plunged its beak into the water and threw its head back, swallowing a small fish or frog.

A group of zebras came to the opposite shore to drink. In the setting sun their white stripes turned to pink. A yellow hornbill landed in the tree above me and started chattering. I tossed it a piece of bread, which to my amazement it caught and swallowed. I threw several more pieces, and it didn't miss one. Its boldness must have been caused by the drought. *"When food is harder to find, their hunger lessens their fear of people.*" The birds in Central Park were always bolder during the winter, especially when there was snow on the ground. I could walk right up to them without their flying. I would have fed the hornbill my entire loaf of bread, but he flew away.

I turned back to the zebras just in time to see a lioness dash into the middle of the group. The zebras ran in every direction. Some of them splashed across the shallow water to my side of the river. Another lioness appeared from nowhere, and together they picked out one zebra and chased it down the riverbed. In seconds they were on it and pulled it down. It kicked and struggled, but the lions overpowered it quickly. I couldn't believe what I had just seen. They tugged and pulled the dead zebra to the shore across from me. A male lion and three more females trotted out of the trees and joined the two females at the carcass. They growled and swatted at each other for a few moments, then settled down to their meal. The other zebras stood and watched the lions, then casually wandered back to where they had been drinking, not fifty feet from where the lions were devouring their herd member, as if nothing had happened.

I watched the lions until it was too dark to see across the river. I heard the snap of bones and the lions' growls and grunts through most of the night.

At first light I started off again. The farther south I went, the rougher the land became. In one place I had to ride around a large hill that was too steep to climb. The detour took me fifteen miles out of my way and brought me only four miles closer to the Nguruman Escarpment.

That afternoon, my stomach began to cramp. I

got off the bike and took a drink of water, hoping that the cramp was caused by thirst. I soon realized it wasn't.

"*Your worst enemy is dehydration, and nothing dehydrates you more than diarrhea.*" I squatted above the river for two hours. I'd been careful with my water. Maybe it was the food. Maybe I had pushed myself too hard.

I rode on for another forty-five minutes, then had to stop again. An hour later, I was on my way again, but I had to stop after only fifteen minutes. I finished my second bottle of water, and I was still very thirsty. I was in trouble. It wasn't lions or leopards that would kill me in Africa—it was microscopic bacteria.

I started a fire, then climbed down to the river and filled the bottles with stagnant water. When I got back up to camp I used my T-shirt as a strainer and poured the water into the pot and put it on the fire. I put the tablets in and let it boil for a long time. After it cooled I poured the water into a bottle and was surprised to see that the straining and boiling had turned two bottles of water into less than one. "*Survival is more important than getting there. . . .*" I climbed back down to the river and repeated the process. Before sunset, I drank one of the bottles of water and repeated the process again.

The next morning, I was thirsty and very weak. I still had diarrhea. I drank a bottle of water and forced myself to eat some food even though I wasn't hungry. None of it did any good; I didn't have enough strength to travel. I would have to stay where I was until I recovered.

Thirteen

I strung my sleeping bag between two trees so that I'd have shade to sit under. It didn't feel any cooler but at least it kept the sun off. I drank both bottles of water, then took the empty bottles and a soup can to the river.

On my side of the river, the bank was at least a dozen feet above the riverbed and I had to slide on my butt most of the way down—a very unpleasant experience when you're having intestinal problems.

I didn't want to drink the water in the stagnant pool. Instead, I used the elephants' technique. With my soup can I dug a hole in the dirt until I hit water, then scooped it out and poured it into the bottles. This took a long time, and the heat sapped my strength. I wondered if I was using more fluid than I was gaining.

By the time I got back to camp I was exhausted. I boiled the water. After it cooled, I drank half of it and fell into a restless sleep.

I dreamed that I was standing next to a large cornfield. My cousin Myron was carrying a baseball bat in one hand and a kachina doll in the other. Grinning, he threw the kachina up into the air, and when it came down he swung the bat and hit the doll over the green field of corn. Taw walked out from the cornstalks and pointed up at the sky, laughing. I looked up and saw gray thunderheads above the field. The sky got very dark, and lightning flashed. I heard my mother call my name, and I started to run. I looked behind and saw that Taw was chasing me. He didn't have a shirt on, and the snake amulet was hanging around his neck. He was gaining on me. I couldn't seem to go any faster. He reached out and grabbed my shirt and started to pull me down. I was terrified. . . .

When I opened my eyes I continued to feel a tugging on my shirt. Groggily, I turned my head in the direction of the tug and saw that the tugger was a vulture! I screamed and swung, missing the bird entirely. The vulture hopped a few feet away and stared at me through black beady eyes mounted on its ugly featherless head.

"I'm not dead!" I yelled.

Another vulture landed near the first.

"I'm not dead!" I yelled again, and picked up the empty soup can and threw it at them. They hopped a few feet away. I got up and ran at them. "Get out of here! I'm not dead!"

They flew off and I dropped to my knees. All my strength was gone. Did the vultures know something that I didn't know? Was I just a corpse to them? I looked at my arms—they were badly burnt. I touched my face. My lips were swollen, and it stung when I touched them. I was too weak to walk, let alone ride my bike. What was I going to do?

You're dehydrated, Jake. You need water. That's the problem. All you need is a little water. . . .

I stumbled back to my camp and thirstily drank what little water I had. It didn't help much. You need more water, Jake.

I went to the edge of the bank, slid down to the

riverbed, and submerged the two bottles into the scummy water. *This water is probably all right to drink. You're sick anyway, it can't get any worse, and if you don't drink you're going to die.* I put the bottle to my lips.

"No!" I yelled. "You've got to boil this stuff first! You've got to put the tablets in it!"

I clawed my way back up the bank and stumbled to the camp. I gathered more wood for the fire and got it going again. With shaking hands I poured the water into the pot and put it on the fire. I dropped in the tablets and watched it boil.

Before it had cooled, I took a sip and burned my lips and tongue. Slow down, Jake! Take it easy! Do you want those ugly birds to tear the flesh off your bones?

I set the pot down and waited for it to cool.

I tested the water with my finger. It was cool enough. Drink half of it, Jake. No matter how you feel, drink half. I swallowed half the water, then put the pot under the map where I wouldn't have to look at it. Out of sight, out of mind. And I thought I *was* going out of my mind. At the survival school they talked about what it was like to die of thirst. *"Things are blown out of proportion, and you become very disoriented. You lose track of where you are. You'll have hallucinations, seeing people and other things that aren't there. Paranoia is common. It's important to try to concentrate on who you are and what you are doing."*

"My name is Jacob Lansa," I said out loud. "I'm in Africa looking for my father. His name is Robert Lansa. He's a field biologist working for . . . Working for . . . He works for . . . My name is Jacob Lansa. I live in . . . I live in . . . Nebraska! No . . . I live in . . . I live in . . . My name is . . . Where'd I put the water? I know I had more water. Where is it? Calm down. Lean back, close your eyes, and rest. This will pass. . . ."

Sometime later, my eyes snapped open. I wasn't sure whether I had been asleep or whether I had passed out. It was dark. The only light came from the coals of the fire. I was wide awake. Something made me open my eyes. It wasn't the nightmare of Taw chasing me. It wasn't a vulture pulling at my clothes. I smelled the smoke of the fire. I listened. In the darkness I heard what sounded like animals running—waves of pounding hooves on the ground. The sound got louder. A loud pitiful shriek broke through the darkness from the direction of the riverbed. I sat up and the world started to spin. I put my hands on the ground to stop myself from falling back. I was shaking with weakness. I took a deep breath trying to rid myself of the dizziness. Smoke! And it wasn't coming from the campfire.

I began to choke. Thick gray smoke swirled all around me. I couldn't stop coughing. I got to my feet and found that it was worse standing. I dropped back to my knees. A reddish light appeared behind me, then I heard a loud crackling sound. Brush fire! A terrified animal rushed past me. Then another and another. They were running from the fire toward the riverbed. I got to my knees just in time to see an elephant dashing blindly toward me. I fell back down, curled into a ball, and covered my head with my arms. The ground vibrated as the elephant ran by, inches from where I lay.

I got to my feet and began to run. I couldn't breathe—it was like being underwater. Smoke, fire, and animals were all around me. Something hit me and I fell. I got back up and stumbled forward, then I was falling. I hit the ground hard, and all the air was pushed out of my lungs. And then there was nothing.

I felt warm and peaceful. The sun was out, but I wasn't hot. I wasn't thirsty. There was no pain. I was floating above the riverbed. Beneath me were dozens of animals. Some were dead and others were alive, writhing in agony, their legs shattered, unable to carry them out of the riverbed. Vultures, jackals, and hyenas were everywhere feasting on the dead and dying animals. Beyond the riverbed, the land had been blackened by the fire.

I looked directly below and saw myself. My eyes were open, staring at nothing because there was nothing left in the shell that was once me. It was me, but it wasn't me, because I was here above the river. The body called silently to me. I knew that I could dive back into it, but I didn't want to, because there would be pain, thirst, diarrhea, and confusion. Above the river there was none of that. I felt weightless and happy. The scavengers hadn't gotten to my carcass yet, but it was only a matter of time. All of us in the riverbed would be picked clean, and when the long rains came our bones would be washed out to sea.

I began to float away from the riverbed. Slowly at first, then with great speed, I sailed over the land. I came to a sudden stop above a giant baobab tree. Below the tree was a huge pile of stones. About a mile away from the tree was a cliff. I floated toward it. Along the cliff was a wide, steep path that led up to a cave opening. Ancient petroglyphs were painted on the wall outside of the cave. I was wondering why I had been brought to this spot when I saw that one of the petroglyphs was similar to the snake design of Taw's amulet—a snake eating its tail. Were the Hopi in Africa? Perhaps I'd floated to Arizona—but there were no baobabs in Arizona. As I thought about this I sailed away again and came to a stop at the riverbed.

The scene below me was the same, except now there was a man—a Masai—standing over my body. When I stopped, he slowly turned and looked directly up to where I was floating, as if he could see me. Was he dead, too? I looked at the riverbed and saw that his presence had disturbed the scavengers. The vultures, jackals, and hyenas all stood at a safe distance watching him. He wore a shuka and carried a spear in his right hand. His hair was short, and it wasn't caked with the red mud of a young warrior. He continued to look up at me.

I opened my mouth to speak, but no words came out. A warm white light appeared above me. In the middle of the light was an iridescent blue opening. From beyond the opening I heard a voice. It sounded like my mother calling. I couldn't understand what she was saying, but I knew that she was inviting me through the opening. I wanted to go to her, but I hesitated. I looked down at my body. When I turned back I saw that the opening was growing smaller and smaller. I didn't know which way to go. Then the opening disappeared. The decision was made for me. I closed my eyes and felt myself falling.

Pain and thirst enveloped me. I opened my eyes and saw the Masai now standing above me.

"Jambo," I croaked through my parched lips.

"Mazuri," he said. "Rest."

I closed my eyes.

Fourteen

I opened my eyes. It was dark out, and I was lying next to a small fire. I tried to raise my head and found that I couldn't. For a moment I thought I was paralyzed. I flexed my fingers—they seemed to be working. I brought my hand to my face and touched it. I tried to move my head again and was able to get it about an inch off the ground. A searing pain shot through my neck and exploded in my head. I eased it back down, relieved that I could move it.

I lifted my head and saw the face of the Masai from my dream. He looked concerned.

"Who . . . ," I began.

"Quiet," the Masai said. "You must rest."

"Who . . . ," I began again.

"Please," he said. "No words. You must not speak. I will talk, but you must be quiet."

He squatted next to me and cradled my head in his hand. "Drink a little." He put a gourd to my lips and let a small amount of water trickle into my mouth. It was a wonderful sensation. "That is enough for now," he said, taking the gourd away.

He sat down across from me. "My name is Supeet," he said. "You have been here for two days."

Two days, I thought. How had forty-eight hours passed without my knowing it? Had I been lying here all that time?

"I found you in the river with the animals."

I remembered the fire and the river. I also remembered floating above my body, the white light, the blue opening, my mother's voice. What was all that about? What had happened to me?

He continued. "I followed your bicycle tracks for two days. I was curious about you. A boy on a bike in the bush is most unusual."

Stupid would be another name for it, I thought.

"When you are stronger," he said, "I will give you food. Until then you must rest and gather your strength."

I closed my eyes and drifted off. Images began to appear. My mother in her coffin. The boxes in our apartment. My father walking through Central Park. Taw sitting by the stream. The amulet. Floating above Africa. The cave. It was like a crazy slide show of unrelated events, but they were all somehow connected. Like road signs, they seemed to be leading me somewhere.

It was light out, and I knew it was late afternoon because of the intense heat. I felt stronger, and with some effort I was able to sit up. The Masai was nowhere to be seen. I had a vague recollection that he had told me his name, but I couldn't remember what it was. I looked around the camp, which was in a small grove of charred trees. I thought about getting up and looking for my bicycle and gear, but my body wouldn't cooperate. I guessed I wouldn't be running around for a while. I was sore, but my stomach and bowels actually felt like they were on the mend. In fact, I realized I was actually hungry.

The Masai appeared from behind the trees and walked into camp. When he saw me sitting up his face broke into a smile.

"You are better," he said.

I managed a little smile in return. "Yeah—I guess."

Over his shoulder he carried the hindquarter of a small antelope. He dropped it by the fire. "You must be thirsty."

"Yes," I said. "And hungry."

A water gourd hung from a leather strap slung over his shoulder. He took if off and handed it to me.

"First you must drink," he said. "Drink slowly and only a small amount."

I took out the stopper and put the gourd to my lips, but I didn't drink. I wondered where he had gotten the water. All I needed was another case of diarrhea. The first bout had almost killed me.

"Drink," he said.

"I don't mean to be impolite," I said. "But where did this water come from?"

The question surprised him. "From the river," he said.

"I'm not sure I can drink it."

He looked down at me and smiled. "You have been drinking it for two days."

I still wasn't convinced. "I have water purification tablets with my gear," I said. "It takes bacteria out of the water so I won't get sick." I was certain that he wouldn't understand this. I was wrong.

He laughed and said, "The water is good. I have added my own purification." Strung on his belt was a small leather bag. He took this off and opened it.

Inside was some fine brown powder. "Go ahead," he said. "Taste it."

I dipped my finger into the bag and put it in my mouth. It was sweet. "What is it?" I asked.

"The bark of a tree and some dried plants," he said. "We use it for many things. It is good for your health. Like a vitamin. Drink."

I believed him. I tipped the gourd back and felt the cool water flow down my throat. It sure tasted good.

"We will eat," he said, sitting down near the hindquarter.

"What is it?"

"Thompson's gazelle."

"Did you kill it with your spear?"

"No," he said. "I borrowed it."

"What do you mean 'borrowed it'?"

"When you are stronger I will show you what I mean," he said.

I wondered if he had gotten it out of the riverbed. The meat couldn't be good after all these days. "My body isn't used to what your body is used to," I said.

"It will be soon," he said, and picked up the hindquarter. He drew a knife from a sheath beneath his shuka and expertly stripped the skin from the leg. He sharpened both ends of a stick and ran it length-wise through the meat of the leg. He jammed one end into the ground near the fire and leaned the stick over the coals.

"I forgot your name," I said.

"Supeet."

"And you're a Masai?"

"Yes," he said.

"I dreamed that I was floating above you in the riverbed," I said.

"That was not a dream."

"It had to be," I insisted.

"What else did you see?" he asked.

I told him about the cave and the petroglyph that looked like my snake amulet.

"May I see the amulet?"

I took it off and handed it to him. He looked at it carefully in the light of the fire.

"Where did you get this?"

"It's from the Hopi Indian tribe," I told him. "It belonged to my grandfather."

"It is very interesting," he said, handing it back. "What is your name?"

"Jacob Lansa."

"And you are Hopi?"

"Half," I said. "You know about the Hopi?"

"I have read about them, yes."

I was startled by this. "Your English is great—where did you learn it?"

"In a mission, then in Nairobi, and later, at university," he said. "You look surprised."

"I am."

"I have a master's degree in philosophy," he said.

"But why—"

"First," he interrupted. "Tell me about yourself. What brings you to Kenya?"

I told him about my mother and father, Sam, my grandfather, Nebraska, the diarrhea, the fire—everything. While I talked he didn't take his eyes off me. He seemed very interested in my story.

When I finished he continued to look at me in

silence. I grew uncomfortable in his steady gaze. By now the meat was sizzling over the fire and smelled wonderful. My mouth began to water.

Finally he said, "Perhaps you are here for other reasons aside from seeing your father."

I thought about this for a moment. If there were other reasons, I didn't know what they were. "What, for instance?" I asked.

"It is difficult to know at this point," he said, taking the stick from the fire. With his knife, he sliced a piece of meat and handed it to me. I ate it greedily—it was incredible.

We both ate for a while without talking. After I finished my third piece of meat, I asked him what he was doing out here.

"I belong here," he said.

"I don't understand."

He laughed. "I'm not sure that I understand, either," he said. "There are many things that I don't understand. And there are many things that you don't understand."

I couldn't argue with him on that issue. It seemed like the older I got, the less I understood what was going on.

"When I was a child," he said, "I wanted to go to the mission school. I did well in school, and because of this I was sent to other schools in the city. When I finished school in Nairobi I returned to my kraal. My family was not the same, nor were the other Masai. They had lost their way. They opened the kraal to tourists who took pictures and wandered around our homes. The cattle herd was now for show. Instead of watching the cattle, the youngsters watched for the dust of the tourist minivans, and the girls would go out onto the road with bare breasts and entice the vans to stop at the kraal. The drivers paid the village money to let the tourists in. Tourists were the new cattle and sheep, and we lost our connection with the land.

"I discovered that there was something missing from my life and perhaps from the life of the Masai. I traveled until I found a tribe of people that still lived in the traditional way. They accepted me, and I lived as they lived for more than a year. They taught me about what was missing."

"And what was that?" I asked.

"A sense of community," he said.

Supeet stood up and gathered more wood for the fire. I'd been so engrossed in what he was saying that I hadn't noticed that the sun had set. He put the wood on the fire and sat back down.

"Why did you leave that tribe if you were happy there?" I asked.

"Because they were not my people. I came back here. There are still a few who believe in the old ways. Not as many as there used to be, but some. I wanted to see what I could do to bring my people back to the land."

I asked him what he meant by the old ways.

"The Masai have many traditions," he said. "For example, when the cattle are happy so are the Masai. We wander with the cattle. The cattle lead us to places we haven't been before. So, in a sense, the cattle are our leaders. Traditionally the Masai like nothing better than to watch the cattle grazing on the green grass. We take pleasure in looking at their bodies, watching the swish of their tails and the tossing of their heads. We find beauty in the smallest detail of their behavior and write songs and poems and dance in honor of them. The cattle are good and useful, and we are happy that they are in our lives. When we look at them we see a power greater than our own."

I told him about my brief visit to the Masai kraal and the poor condition of the cattle I saw there.

"Yes," he said. "Many cattle have died. But there is good in the drought. It has brought some of the people back to the old ways. Seeing the death and suffering has brought a few Masai back to themselves."

He paused a moment, picked up a stick from the fire, and looked at the flame. "Some Masai believe that we have lost our spirit and therefore we are being punished."

"Do you believe this?"

"Yes," he said. "Bad luck is always brought on by a failure of the spirit of one kind or another."

"What did you mean by community?" I asked.

"Community is as important as food, shelter, and water," he said. "Without community there is little use for the other necessities of life.

"Technology brings comfort, but it can also undermine our dealings with people. Some might look at me and say that I have nothing, but if I have community I have everything."

I shook my head. I was still confused.

"Community is not just people," he said. "It is everything around you. You think that you have seen Kenya, but Kenya has seen more of you than you have of it. You have ridden over the land, but you have not seen it."

"But who has time to see in this way?" I asked.

"Those who take the time," he said.

I thought about this as he put more sticks on the fire, then realized that I hadn't thanked him for saving my life.

"If you hadn't found me," I said, "I would have died."

He shrugged his shoulders. "Who's to say what would have happened? You are young, and you have a mission. A goal makes one strong. It is a tool that can be used to help you through bad times."

"I don't think it was a goal that saved my life," I said. "It was you."

"Perhaps," he said.

"So what's your goal, Supeet?"

"To make it rain," he said.

"You're trying to make it rain now?"

"I am fulfilling what must be done until I arrive at the place where the rains are made."

"And where is that?"

He pointed south. "There is only one man who knows exactly where it is. He is an old Masai named Sitonik—a *Laibon*."

"A Laibon?" I asked.

"A spiritual leader to the Masai. An enchanter, witch doctor, sorcerer—it means many different things. I must see Sitonik. If the long rains fail, the cattle will die and so will the Masai."

"Why you?" I asked.

"It is why I am here," he said.

"Your purpose?"

"One of them."

"And you believe that you can make it rain?"

"I believe you can make anything happen if you

truly believe that it will happen." He looked up at the sky. "It is dark and the cicada are out. In Masailand we say that the day is for people, and the night is for wild animals. It is time to sleep."

He curled up next to the fire and closed his eyes. I looked at him for a long time. My mind raced with questions.

"Supeet?"

He opened his eyes.

"Will you help me find my father's camp?"

He smiled, then closed his eyes again without answering my question.

Fifteen

The following morning I woke up at dawn. Supeet was curled up on the other side of the campfire's gray ashes, still asleep. Quietly, I got to my feet. My legs were still shaky, so I stood there for a few minutes giving them a chance to recall what their job was.

The camp was near where I had fallen into the riverbed. Unsteadily, I made my way to the nearest tree and relieved myself, then walked to the edge of the riverbed. The smell was horrible, but nothing compared to what I saw over the edge. Dozens of bloated carcasses were strewn over the riverbed, most of them partially eaten. Vultures, marabou storks, jackals, hyenas, and millions of flies gorged on the rotting flesh. When I was lying by the fire I had wondered why the flies were not buzzing around me. Now I knew—they were busy elsewhere. I pulled my T-shirt up over my nose and stared at the carnage. *That could be you down there, Jake.* I thought again about floating above the riverbed and the blue light and how detached I had felt from what was happening below me.

I turned away from the riverbed and tried to get my bearings. I wanted to find my old camp and get my gear. About a hundred yards away I saw the tree I had used as a sun shelter. I walked over to it.

The fire had done its work. The panniers and everything in them were destroyed. The only things left were the metal frames and a couple of charred cans of food. I picked up my melted bicycle helmet and angrily threw it toward the river. What are you going to do now, Jake? What are you going to do? All I had was the box of matches in my pocket.

I looked down at the gear again and noticed that my bike wasn't there. I looked around and didn't see it anywhere. By some miracle had it been saved? I hurried back to Supeet's camp—perhaps he had moved it.

Supeet was awake, sitting by the fire chewing on a piece of meat.

"My bike!" I said breathlessly. "Did you move it?"

He looked at me calmly and continued to chew until he swallowed. "Yes," he said.

"Then it's not wrecked?"

"Come," he said, standing up. "I'll show you."

He led me to an acacia tree not far from camp. My bike was gently swinging from the lowest branch. All that was left were the charred frame and the tire rims. So much for miracles, I thought. And I was just getting used to the zebra stripes.

"How did it get in the tree?" I asked.

"I hung it there."

"Why?" I asked in disbelief.

Supeet shrugged his shoulders. "Something to do," he said.

I looked at him, then back to the bike. A fitting grave for a gallant steed.

"That was everything I had," I said.

"Not everything." Supeet pointed to the base of the tree.

The kachina doll was leaning against the trunk without a scorch mark on it. I picked it up.

"This is made from cottonwood," I said. "It should have burned up in the fire."

"Fire cannot destroy spirits," Supeet said.

"Kachinas *represent* spirits," I said. "They aren't spirits themselves."

"Then why didn't it burn in the fire?" Supeet asked, and walked away.

I examined the kachina carefully. *"Kachinas know how to take care of themselves. They like to travel."* Maybe Taw was right.

I walked back to camp. Supeet was kicking dirt over the ashes of the fire. "You seem somewhat recovered," he said. "Sitonik's kraal is on the way to your father's camp. Perhaps we should walk together."

I put the kachina in my pocket, and we headed south along the riverbed.

As we walked, there seemed to be more animals than before. The zebras, giraffes, and bush bucks glanced at us as we passed, then went back to their grazing as if we weren't there. I mentioned this to Supeet.

"The animals have always been here," he said. "I suspect that you frightened them with your bike. If you want to see the animals you must move in sympathy with the land. When you learn to see as the animals see your fear goes away, and the animals no longer fear you."

Later we passed a small herd of elephants in the riverbed. Supeet pointed to a small calf nursing from its mother. "That one is no more than a couple of weeks old," he said. "The Masai have great respect for elephants. If a herder sees an elephant near a kraal he will bring the cattle home at dusk. If he hears an elephant trumpet he will pay it tribute by ringing the cow-bells. If you find the afterbirth of an elephant, very good fortune will come your way."

"Do you really believe that?" I asked.

"Finding the afterbirth is rare," he said. "A cere-mony is performed, and it can take a while for the good fortune to mature, but yes, I do believe it. I knew a family outside of Narok who were very poor until their son found the afterbirth. They are now the wealthiest family in the area."

"But did it really have anything to do with the afterbirth?"

"Yes," he said. "It did."

He stopped, slipped the water gourd from his shoulder, and handed it to me. I took a long drink. I didn't know what to believe about an elephant's after-birth, but I did know that the powder Supeet used in the water seemed to have cured my problem. As far as I was concerned that was very good fortune. He had stopped twice to fill the gourd. With the powder we had an endless supply of water. I handed the gourd back to him.

He took a drink, then stood for a moment looking off in the distance. "What do you see?" he asked.

"Where?"

"In front of us."

I saw a kopje, which is a small hill covered with large boulders. Fifty yards away were two acacia trees. There was a termite mound near the bank of the river. The landscape looked the same as it had for several hours.

"I don't see anything," I said.

"I will teach you to see," he said. "It will take you

some time to understand and perhaps you never will. That is up to you."

"I'm willing to learn," I said.

"Good," Supeet said. "You must first stop looking at things the way you have looked at them in the past. You must see things with new eyes. The land has a language of its own and to see you must understand that language. There is a difference between seeing something the first time and seeing it the second time. For instance, when you come to a town that you have not seen before you pay close attention. The second time you go to that town you see less because you look at what is familiar."

I hadn't thought about this before, but what he was saying was true. The train from New York City to Poughkeepsie passed through many towns. The first time I made the trip with my parents I paid close attention. I'd look at buildings and houses, wondering what was going on inside them. The second and third trips, I paid less attention to what was passing by. On the last trip to see Taw I had barely glanced out the window.

"I think I understand," I said.

Supeet continued. "Each time you see something, no matter how familiar you are with it, try to see it as if it were new. Try to pick out what has changed since you saw it last. Nothing stays the same—it may look the same, but it is always different. The reason it looks the same is because you are looking at your memory of it—not at what it is."

"Seeing this way would be difficult," I said.

"And no one sees perfectly," Supeet added. "We take seeing for granted. To see well takes practice, and it can take a whole lifetime to learn. So don't worry about understanding now. There is no hurry."

He walked on and stopped closer to the acacia trees. He pointed at one of the trees. "What do you see?"

I stared at the tree for a moment. "I see an acacia tree," I said.

"There is something else there." Supeet reached down, picked up a stick, and threw it at the tree. A leopard jumped to the ground, snarled, then bounded away from us.

"How could I have missed it!" I said. "And why did it run away?"

"Leopards are smart," Supeet said. "They'd rather escape than fight."

"But how did you know it was there?"

Supeet smiled. "I knew a predator was near because there are fewer animals. The behavior of animals can tell you much about what is going on around you."

"Look at the white space, Jake. Sometimes it's the things we can't see and don't hear that are the most important." It seemed that Supeet and my father spoke the same language.

"My father has said the same thing."

"Then he knows something about how to see," Supeet said.

"You and my father would get along well," I said. In fact, being with Supeet was a lot like being with my father.

"Are you hungry?" he asked.

"Yes," I said.

"Then we will make camp here and eat."

"Eat what?"

"Come with me."

I followed him away from the riverbed. We walked by a kopje. On the other side the land opened up into a broad expanse of savanna. Supeet slowed his pace and looked as though he was concentrating on everything around him. Suddenly he crouched down and motioned for me to do the same.

"Stay here," he whispered.

I watched as he slowly crept forward—sometimes crouching, sometimes standing erect. At times he would freeze and stay perfectly still for several minutes. It took him at least fifteen minutes to get a hundred yards away. Suddenly, without warning, Supeet jumped up from a crouch and let out a blood-curdling scream that almost made me wet my pants. He ran forward with his spear in the air, and I saw a cheetah bolt across the savanna. The cheetah stopped after about a hundred yards and looked back to where Supeet was standing.

"You can come now," Supeet yelled to me.

I stood and jogged over to him.

"Dinner," he said.

Laying at his feet was a Grant's gazelle. I squatted down and touched it—it was still warm.

"We will borrow a leg," Supeet said. "The cheetah will not mind. There is more meat here than it can eat anyway." Expertly, he cut a hindquarter off with his sheath knife.

I looked in the direction of the cheetah. The beautiful cat sat patiently staring at us. I expected it to defend its kill.

"Don't worry about the cheetah," Supeet said. "It

will come back and finish its dinner when we are gone."

"Is this how you got the meat last night?" I asked.

"Of course," he said. "You thought I took the meat from the riverbed, didn't you?"

"Yes," I said sheepishly.

Supeet laughed. "You must have been hungry to eat what you thought was unclean meat."

"I was starving," I said. "Is this how you get all of your meat?"

"Most of the time. There are other ways of course, but this is the easiest."

"Always from cheetahs?"

"No," Supeet said, picking up the hindquarter. "There are many predators in Africa."

"How do you know where to look?"

"Imagine that you are a large cat. Where would you wait for your food?"

"At watering holes," I said. "I've seen lions do this."

"That's a good place to start looking," Supeet said. "I knew of this cheetah because I've hunted here before. I saw the group of gazelles running, and I could tell by how they ran that a cheetah was chasing them. When they stopped, I knew the cheetah had been successful. Once the cheetah killed, there was no longer any reason for the gazelles to run."

Just like the zebras I had seen in the riverbed. After the lions pulled one down the threat was over. Life goes on.

"Are there other ways of getting meat?"

"There is another way that you might be interested in," Supeet said. "Perhaps if there is time tomorrow, I will show you."

*   *   *

That night, as I was falling asleep, I thought about the things that Supeet had taught me. I also thought about my father. I was now confident that I would find his camp, but finding it did not seem as urgent as it had a few days before.

Sixteen

When I woke, Supeet was gone and the heat was already stifling. I stood up and looked around. Where had he gone? Maybe he'd wandered off to relieve himself or to borrow breakfast. Perhaps, but what if he didn't come back? Then what would I do? I walked a short distance from camp but still didn't see him. I called out his name a few times, but there was no response. I was worried and uncomfortable, and I carried these feelings back to camp. I sat down near the fire.

"Did you call?"

I jumped and turned to see Supeet laughing at my startled reaction.

"Yeah," I said. I was relieved and embarrassed.

"I wouldn't leave without saying good-bye," he said. "That would be impolite."

"I'm glad to hear that," I said.

Supeet sat down. "This is a good place for me to show you another technique for getting close to animals," he said. "Once perfected it can be used in many situations."

"Sure." My body was tired and sore, and a little break from walking would do it good. I felt that my best bet was to stick close to Supeet no matter what he wanted to do. I was beginning to feel very comfortable with him, and I wanted to learn as much as I could before we parted ways.

"I must warn you though," he said. "It will take several hours, which will delay our arrival to the Nguruman Escarpment."

"By how long?" I asked.

"By a day, at least. We will not finish until dark, and we will have to camp here again tonight."

"How far are we from my father's camp?"

"Two days," he said. "Perhaps more. It depends on where your father is. The Nguruman Escarpment is a large area, and it's difficult to say how long it will take to find his camp."

"Then you're going to help me find my father?" I asked. I was more than willing to give up a day if Supeet would help me.

"First, I must see the old Laibon, Sitonik. Then I'll know if there is time to help you."

"When will you see him?"

"I think tomorrow," Supeet said.

"I'm not so worried about time anymore," I said.

He smiled. "Good! You are making progress. Come with me."

He led me to a tree not far from the camp.

"You must climb as high as you can and find a comfortable branch where you can look out over the savanna." He handed me the water gourd. "You will need this."

I took the gourd. "What about you?"

"I will be too busy to drink," he said.

I didn't know what he meant by this, but I climbed the bone-dry tree anyway and found a large branch near the top that was comfortable.

"Can you see the grass of the savanna?" Supeet yelled up to me.

"Yes," I shouted back.

"Good! What else do you see?"

Here we go again, I thought. I looked carefully. Shimmering waves of heat created mirages in the distance. I saw three kopjes within a half mile of each other. Trees dotted the landscape, and there were several small groups of animals grazing on the dry grass of the savanna. About a hundred and fifty yards away, a herd of zebras took advantage of the shade of an acacia tree. A few hundred feet past the herd were a few more trees and underneath them were two rhinoceroses sleeping. I told Supeet what I saw.

"Watch me," he said. "And remember this will take some time. If you lose track of where I am, look to the zebras and work your way back to where you last saw me."

"I will," I said, still confused about what was going on.

Supeet walked briskly out into the savanna, then stopped. He slipped off his sandals and shuka, then reached down for something I couldn't quite see and rubbed it all over his body. When he was finished he lay down and rolled on the ground, then got back to his feet. From head to toes he was covered with red dust and blended in perfectly with his surroundings.

For several minutes he stood perfectly still, looking at the zebras beneath the acacia tree, then he began to move very slowly in their direction. His movements reminded me of the mimes I had seen in Central Park. Each step was exaggerated and painfully slow. Sometimes he froze in midstep, holding his leg up for several minutes, before putting his foot gently on the ground. The closer he got to the zebras the slower he went. Twice I took my eyes off him and had trouble finding him again.

When he was twenty-five feet away from the zebras they still gave no sign that they knew he was there. It was incredible! They swished their tails at flies and looked out over the savanna as if nothing were happening. I waited for Supeet to rush in on them, but instead, he moved even more slowly. In fact, the only way I could tell he was moving was by looking at the spot he had previously occupied. He literally inched his way toward them. I wondered how long it had taken him to perfect this technique. If Supeet could make himself essentially invisible, he could do just about anything—including make it rain.

Finally, he was close enough to one zebra to touch it. Which he did, slapping it on the butt. The zebras jumped around in confusion, then in panic bolted across the savanna. Supeet stood under the acacia laughing at the joke he had played on them.

I climbed down and jogged over to him. When I got up to him I told him that it was the most amazing thing I had ever seen.

"It's actually a game," he said. "When we were boys we practiced with rhinoceroses when they were asleep. The first boy places a rock on the rhinoceros's back without waking it. The next boy takes the first boy's rock and places his own rock on the back and so on, until someone makes a mistake and wakes the rhinoceros."

And my parents used to worry about some of the things my friends and I did in New York City!

"It's great fun," Supeet said. "Until the animal wakes up, that is." He laughed. "Rhinoceroses are easy. Rhinoceroses have few enemies and are not as alert as animals that are preyed upon. The tribe taught me to stalk many other animals."

"You must be exhausted," I said.

"I could use a drink of water."

I handed him the gourd, and he took a long drink.

"Would you like to learn?"

"Yes!"

"All right," he said. "But by the time we finish, it will be too late to travel."

"I don't care."

"Good! We will stalk the rhinoceroses by those trees. Try not to wake them, though."

Good safety tip, I thought.

"Take your clothes and shoes off," he said.

"My shoes, too?" I protested. "There are thorns on the ground."

Supeet said, "The thorns will make you move slowly. Do animals wear shoes?"

"I get the point," I said. "No pun intended." I took off my tennis shoes and clothes.

Supeet wandered away for a moment and came back with a plant he had uprooted. "Rub this all over yourself," he said. "Including your hair."

I did as he asked until I was covered with a sticky residue.

"Now lie down and cover yourself with dust."

When I stood up Supeet and I were the exact same color. He looked at me and grinned.

"The first rule," he said, "is that you are not allowed to look at the ground. The second rule is never take your eyes off your goal. If you move slowly enough your feet will see the ground. If you feel that you are about to step on something unpleasant move your foot until there is something pleasant to step on. The third rule is to move toward the wind when possible. It will blow your scent behind you."

He demonstrated by walking very slowly away from the acacia.

"It is very tiring," he said. "After we reach the rhinoceroses we will have to move away from them in the same manner so we do not disturb them. Let's go."

We began the stalk. It wasn't easy. At first I watched Supeet out of the corner of my eye as I approached the rhinos. Sweat began to pour off me. Twice I stepped on thorns, which taught me to be more careful.

After a while I began to develop a rhythm, and this made it easier. The only thing that mattered was getting to the rhinos undetected. I lost track of time. I was surprised at how aware I was of everything around me. I wasn't seeing things as much as I was *feeling* them. It was like I had become a part of the sun, air, and land. It was remarkable!

At twenty-five feet I could see the rhinos clearly. I began to move even more slowly. The rhinos were lying about three feet apart. Their thick skin was covered with red dust. A small bird hopped along the back of one of the rhinos pecking at insects.

I saw their nostrils move as they inhaled and exhaled the hot African air. Their ears twitched in response to the buzzing flies. I wished that I had ears to keep the flies off me.

When I was ten feet away it occurred to me that if I could approach without scaring the bird away I would have a better chance of success. I concentrated on the bird's every move. When it stopped I froze. I began to move only when it moved. It seemed totally unaware of me.

Finally, I was within inches of the first rhino. I stayed perfectly still, looking at the gigantic beast, watching its rib cage heave with each breath. This was much different than seeing a rhino in a zoo. These animals were free to come and go as they pleased. The rhinos' only enemies were the poachers that killed them for their horns and left their bodies to rot in the African sun. The horns were ground into powder and sold as aphrodisiacs to stimulate the male sex drive—an Asian myth that many still believed. I knew that if people could see rhinos as I was seeing them now, they would not tolerate the slaughter.

Now that I was right next to them, I didn't know what to do next. Very slowly I turned my head to find Supeet, but he was nowhere to be seen. Where had he gone? Had he disappeared? Was I invisible? Moving only my eyes, I scanned the landscape. I finally saw him standing fifty feet away. At some point he had stopped and backtracked away from the rhinos. I guessed that he wanted me to experience this alone. I smiled at him.

I looked down. Making certain that I was well balanced, I bent slowly forward. The maneuver took a long time, and I came back up just as slowly. The bird was still hopping along the rhino's back.

With the greatest care I reached forward and placed a pebble on the back of the rhinoceros. After I slowly drew my hand away the small bird hopped over to the pebble and pecked at it. I began to inch away from the resting rhinos.

*   *   *

"You did well," Supeet said. "It must be that Hopi blood of yours."

I looked back at the two rhinos still sleeping under the tree. The sun was beginning to sink below the eastern horizon.

"I had a good teacher," I said.

"You taught yourself," he said. "It is the only teacher we pay any real attention to."

As we walked back to camp I wondered what I had missed every day of my life by not paying attention to what was there.

Seventeen

We left early the next morning and walked for several miles. The Nguruman Escarpment was east of us, across the riverbed. I looked at the huge hills in the distance stretching as far as I could see. It wasn't going to be easy to find my father.

As we walked I thought about Taw's dream. *"I saw you walking in a big land. You were not alone, but I could not see who you were with."* I guess his dream had come true—I *was* walking in a big land and I was not alone.

There were times that I had to almost jog to keep up with Supeet, and I suspected that if he was alone he would be moving at an even brisker pace.

He pointed to a column of smoke rising in the distance. "Poachers," he said.

I looked. The smoke came from the other side of a small hill. "How do you know?" I asked.

"I have seen their signs all day," he said. "They have killed something, and it is being cooked."

"I don't understand."

"I will show you," he said. "But we must be careful. They are very dangerous men."

We walked toward the hill and climbed up the steep bank. When we got to the top we crawled the last thirty feet and peeked over the edge.

Below, leaning against an old truck, were four

men carrying rifles. The truck was parked near the carcasses of two elephants. My father's letters had not prepared me for the horror of what I saw. The poachers watched as a group of people butchered the elephants. I heard the steady *thunk . . . thunk . . . thunk* as the axes chopped the ivory tusks. The women took heavy strips of elephant meat and placed them on the fire. Standing next to one of the elephants was a young calf. It nudged its dead mother with its trunk, trying to get her to move. Every once in a while it let out a sorrowful bellow. The people gathering the meat paid little attention to the calf, but the poachers thought it was funny and pointed and laughed at it.

I was enraged. I wanted to kill them. As if he could read my mind, Supeet put his hand on my shoulder. He shook his head sadly and whispered, "There is nothing you can do."

"What about the calf?" I asked angrily.

Supeet shook his head.

I looked on helplessly as one of the poachers walked up behind the calf and kicked it, then ran away laughing. The calf turned and charged. The poacher slipped and fell, but before the calf could reach him, several shots rang out. The impact of the bullets sent the calf cartwheeling, then it crumpled to the ground. I felt myself rising up, but Supeet tightened his grip on my shoulder and pulled me back down.

"No!" he said.

The poachers were laughing. I was stunned.

"We must go now," Supeet whispered. "We have seen enough."

I hesitated.

Supeet whispered more emphatically, "We must go!"

I didn't want to—I wanted to do something! No wonder my father decided to stay behind.

Supeet dragged me away from the edge, and for the first time I was angry with him. "No," I said. "Let me go!" I tried to jerk away, but he held on. How could he watch this senseless slaughter and not want to do something about it? I rolled away from him and stood up. He tackled me and pinned me to the ground. I couldn't move. His face was right next to mine.

"Listen!" he said. "You must get hold of yourself, Jacob. There is nothing we can do about this. We have another goal."

"My goal is to find my father—maybe to help him with his work. Those elephants are why he's out here. I don't know about your goal—"

"Our goals are the same!"

"Your goal is to make it rain. My goal is . . ."

"If it rains, the slaughter may stop."

"*A little rain changes everything—that's the remarkable thing about East Africa. A few days of rain can turn this hard, grim land into a soft green landscape.*"

I understood what Supeet was saying, but I doubted my earlier belief that he could do it.

"Nobody can make it rain," I said bitterly.

Supeet sat up slowly but still held my arm firmly. He looked at the cloudless African sky and said sadly, "You may be right, Jacob. But somebody has to try."

I followed his upward gaze, feeling guilty for what I'd said. I thought about the poachers' cruelty. "Those bastards!"

"Now is not the time," he said, letting my arm go.

I sat for a few moments breathing deeply, feeling the fight drain from me. But the memory of what I had seen would never leave me. Supeet was right; now wasn't the time. I looked at him and knew that he had saved my life again. We stood, brushed ourselves off, and walked down the other side of the hill.

We walked for several hours in silence. I couldn't stop thinking about what the poachers had done. Elephants were murdered for their tusks. The tusks were smuggled out of the country and shipped all over Asia, where the ivory was carved by people as poor as the poachers who had killed the elephants. My father had written to me many times about the illegal ivory trade.

> The export ban on ivory has driven up the price of the white gold. The more difficult something is to obtain, the more expensive it becomes. But what else can they do? Africa is a big place, and every elephant can't be guarded. So they make it illegal to export ivory, and other countries make it illegal to import it. And this brings in a different caliber of poacher with sophisticated weapons, communication, transportation, and money. The greater the risk, the greater the profit. I suppose the slaughter won't end until the last bullet is shot through the heart of the last elephant. . . .

And for what, I thought. So wealthy people can have ivory necklaces and bracelets to wear, or ivory knickknacks to display on their mantels and shelves? What was the point of this?

Supeet broke the silence. "Sitonik is near."

"What?"

"Sitonik is near," Supeet repeated.

"How do you know?" I asked.

Supeet looked at me and smiled. "I feel him. Don't you?"

"No," I said. The only thing I felt was sorrow for the poor elephant calf and its mother, now in the bellies of those people. And outrage over the fact that I hadn't been able to do anything about it.

"You're still angry," Supeet said.

I looked at him. "Not at you," I said. "You did me a favor. I don't know what I was thinking."

"There was nothing the matter with your thinking. Your action could have been a problem, though."

"My mother said that I inherited my father's temper."

"As we get older we become our fathers and mothers. The best we can hope for is to live our lives as well or better then they have."

I thought about this. He was right; our parents *were* inside of us. I carried mine wherever I went. My mother had died, but her life continued with me.

We walked on for a while longer, then Supeet stopped and looked straight ahead.

"What is it?" I didn't see anything unusual.

Suddenly, not twenty feet away, a very old man stepped out from behind a thick clump of bushes. His abrupt appearance startled me. He leaned on a long staff and stared at us.

"Sitonik?" I asked.

Supeet nodded.

Sitonik was very old and frail. Loose skin hung on

his bony frame, giving him a shriveled appearance. He wore a bright red shuka and a very old necklace made out of large blue beads, lions' teeth, and feathers. He smiled and motioned for us to step forward.

Supeet and he exchanged greetings in Masai, then Supeet bent forward and the old man spit on his hand and placed it on Supeet's head.

"You must do the same," Supeet said to me.

I hesitated.

"Go on," Supeet insisted. "It is customary."

I bent forward and felt Sitonik's hand touch my head. When I stood up they exchanged more words, and Sitonik turned and started to walk away.

"He has invited us to his kraal," Supeet said. We followed him.

"Should he be out here alone?"

"There are others back at the kraal. Nobody tells Sitonik what he should be doing." Supeet laughed.

"How old is he?"

"I don't know. Some say that he is the oldest man in Africa. When I was a boy he looked just as he does now. And my father said that Sitonik looked the same when he was a boy."

"Come on, Supeet!" I protested. "Nobody lives that long."

Supeet smiled and continued to walk.

I figured the kraal was close by. I was wrong. Mile after mile we followed Sitonik through the bush. He moved at a slow, steady pace without resting or taking a sip of water. The walk to his kraal was far from easy. He led us over the top of small hills and through very dense brush.

"Was he waiting for us?" I asked.

Supeet nodded.

"How did he know we'd be there?"

"Sitonik is *the* Laibon. It's his job to know these things."

"There are other Laibons?"

"Yes," Supeet said. "But only one Sitonik."

We followed Sitonik for the rest of the day. At sunset we climbed to the top of a hill. On the other side was a typical circular Masai kraal surrounded by a thorn fence. A fire burned in the middle of the kraal, sending up a thin column of smoke into the dusk. A few cattle and goats were secured behind a wooden fence in one part of the kraal.

We followed Sitonik down the hill and through the opening of the kraal. As soon as we got inside, two young boys ran over and pulled a thorn barricade across the entrance.

Aside from the two boys, there were two women in the kraal about Supeet's age. They showed no concern over the fact that Sitonik had been gone for most of the day. And as far as I knew, he could have been gone for several days, or weeks.

We walked over to the fire, and Sitonik said something to one of the women. She went over to the cows, put a rope around one of them, and led it back to the fire. The other woman took a gourd and squirted milk into it from the cow's teat.

A young boy ran up with a miniature bow and arrow and handed them to Sitonik.

The woman holding the rope tightened it around the cow's neck until its jugular vein stood out. Sitonik strung the bow, took aim at the jugular, and let the arrow fly from about three feet away. When the arrow was removed a stream of blood flowed out and the second woman caught it in the milk gourd. When it was full, Sitonik bent down and picked up a piece of dried cow dung, spit on it, then pinched it over the wound. The woman loosened the rope and the bleeding stopped. Throughout this procedure the cow stood calmly, as if nothing had happened.

Sitonik took the gourd and shook it gently and handed it to Supeet. Supeet said something to him, then tilted his head back and poured blood-milk into his mouth. He then handed the gourd to me. The group was watching me. I didn't want to drink the stuff, but I also didn't want to embarrass Supeet.

"Go ahead," Supeet said.

I took a deep breath and held it, put my head back, and filled my mouth with blood-milk. When I swallowed I felt my stomach jump, but nothing came back up—thank God. The warm mixture wasn't bad. In fact I took another drink before handing it back to the now grinning Sitonik, who said something to Supeet.

"He says that you must be Masai."

I smiled at Sitonik. Supeet and Sitonik sat by the fire and motioned for me to do the same. The woman led the cow back to the corral, and the other woman brought us some dried meat to eat. Supeet and Sitonik began an animated conversation that I couldn't understand. I looked up at the sky. The sun had set, and the moon appeared above the kraal, three-quarters full.

The two men talked for hours. Once in a while I tried to figure out what they were saying, but mostly I just looked at the fire and thought about the things that had happened to me during the past several days. I was caught up in something that I didn't fully understand. I now knew that I wasn't in Africa just to find my father. There were other reasons for my coming here. Supeet's arrival at the riverbed was not a lucky coincidence. *"Perhaps you are here for other reasons. . . ."*

The conversation between the two men stopped abruptly. Sitonik stood up and walked into one of the huts. Supeet watched him go.

"What's going on?" I asked.

"He is preparing something for us," Supeet said.

"For us?"

"He says that you are part of this, too."

"Part of what?"

"The rain ceremony is more complicated than I thought," he said.

"Then he told you where the rains are made?"

"Not yet, but he will."

"What's my part in this?" I asked.

"He didn't say. Only that you were a part of it. Perhaps you have already fulfilled your part."

"I haven't done anything!"

Supeet ignored my comment and continued, "The rain ceremony must be performed during the coming full moon. Sitonik says there is no other time that it will work."

"So what's he preparing in the hut?"

"He is going to teach me the ceremony. But first he wants to throw the bones."

"What bones?"

"You'll see," Supeet said. "Throwing the bones is how Sitonik sees into the future. He can read the bones."

Just then Sitonik stuck his head out of the hut and motioned for us to come inside.

"Let's go," Supeet said.

I got up and followed him to the hut. A dog was curled up outside the entrance. On my way in, I reached down to pet it. It whirled around and snapped at my hand. I jumped backward and fell. It wasn't a dog—it was a hyena! It let out a loud eerie cackle and scooted to the other side of the kraal. I looked up at Supeet and Sitonik. They were bent over, howling in laughter. Very funny, I thought. How was I supposed to know it was a hyena? The Masai put up thorn fences to keep hyenas out of kraals! Only a strange old bird like Sitonik would have one for a pet! The two men got themselves under control, only to start laughing again, harder than the first time.

"You should have seen your face, Jacob!" Supeet said in between bouts of laughter.

Sitonik was having a hard time catching his breath. I stood up with as much dignity as I could and brushed myself off. After what seemed an eternity, the laughter subsided.

"Well, that certainly broke the ice," Supeet said. "Would you like to try to come in again?"

I walked past them into the hut. Supeet and Sitonik followed me in, and we all sat by the small fire that burned in the center of the dirt floor.

Sitonik pulled a small bag made of leopard skin out from his shuka. He carefully opened the bag and spilled its contents out on the dirt. Among the bones were several colorful beads, old buttons, coins, pebbles, and a small round amulet with a carved snake eating its tail. It was almost identical to the one Taw had given me. I pointed it out to Supeet, and he said something to Sitonik.

Sitonik talked excitedly for a few moments.

"He wants to see your amulet."

I took it off and handed it to Sitonik. He held it in his gnarled old hand and felt the impression of the snake with his thumb. He said something to Supeet.

"He says that it is not the same, but it is similar. It has power like his, but a different power."

"I don't understand," I said.

Supeet smiled. "It is enough to know that it has power."

Sitonik said something else.

"He says that you should always wear it. That it is like . . . there is not an exact translation. But it is like a body organ—a vital body organ."

I knew exactly what Sitonik was saying. When the amulet wasn't around my neck I felt peculiar—as if something was missing.

"He says that there is something else," Supeet said.

I waited to hear what it was, but Sitonik didn't say anything.

"No," Supeet said. "Something you have with you."

I had no idea what he was talking about. I didn't have anything else—then I remembered the kachina. I pulled it out of my pocket and handed it to Sitonik.

Very gently he took the doll and held it near the fire. Supeet and he had a very long conversation. I guessed that Supeet was explaining to him what the doll meant, because I heard the words "kachina" and "Hopi" several times. When they were finished talking, Sitonik handed the doll back to me. I took it and looked at Supeet.

"He says that the kachina is very important. That

it has come a long way to help us. He will say a blessing to thank it for coming here."

"Tell him that my grandfather thanks him."

Supeet translated and Sitonik smiled.

"Now he's going to throw the bones."

Sitonik scooped up the pile and held it gently in his cupped hands. He said a couple of words, then spit in his hands and let the bones fall to the ground. He looked at the pile for a long time, then nodded and said something to Supeet.

"The bones are happy tonight," Supeet said.

Sitonik picked the pile up and poured it into Supeet's outstretched hands. Supeet went through the same routine, spitting on the bones and letting them drop. Sitonik examined the pile carefully and told Supeet what the bones were saying.

"He says that I am lucky and so are the Masai."

"What about the rain?" I asked.

"The bones said nothing about the rain."

"What does that mean?"

"It means that I am lucky," Supeet said. "Perhaps that is enough to make it rain." He picked the bones up and handed them to me.

"What am I supposed to do?"

"Throw the bones," Supeet said.

"But I don't know what to say."

"Just spit on them and let them drop. The bones know what to do."

I spit and let them go. Sitonik came around to my side of the fire and peered down at the pile. He turned to Supeet and said a few words.

"He says that you are going to have a difficult journey."

"More difficult than I've already had?" I wasn't thrilled to hear this.

"Apparently," Supeet said.

"Great." How about two out of three? I thought.

"He will now show me the rain ceremony, and I will practice."

"Do you want me to leave?"

"No, you may stay."

Sitonik went to another part of the hut and came back with two small zebra-skin drums. He handed one of them to Supeet and sat down next to him with the other drum.

He looked at Supeet to make certain he was paying attention, then he tapped out an intricate pattern on the drum. Supeet listened carefully, and when Sitonik finished, he tried to duplicate the beat. The first couple of times he didn't get it right, and Sitonik corrected him by saying something, then repeating the beat on his own drum. After a few tries, Supeet got the rhythm down, and the two men tapped it out on their drums in unison. Sitonik began to chant, and Supeet joined in.

The drums and the sound of their voices reverberated through the warm hut. I was fascinated by the ceremony and wondered what the words meant, but I couldn't keep my eyes open. I pinched myself a couple of times to keep from falling asleep, but it didn't do any good.

I woke up the next morning lying next to the ashes of the fire. I got up slowly and walked outside.

Supeet and Sitonik were sitting in the center of the kraal talking. Supeet waved when he saw me, then continued his conversation with Sitonik. I walked over to them.

"Did you sleep well?" Supeet asked, standing up.

"I'm not sure. I don't feel very rested."

"It was probably the drums." He helped Sitonik to his feet. "It is time for us to go," he said, and they started walking away.

I followed behind. One of the women ran over and gave me a handful of dried meat. I thanked her and put the meat in my pocket.

Sitonik stood near the entrance and said a few words. Supeet bowed forward; Sitonik spit on his hand and put it on Supeet's head. Sitonik turned to me and said the same words, and when he was finished I bent forward. I figured that he was saying good-bye or giving us some kind of blessing. Sitonik then reached into his shuka and pulled out the bag of bones. He said a few more words, then handed the bag to Supeet. Supeet looked shocked. He held the bag in his hand and stared at Sitonik. His eyes misted over, and tears began rolling down his face. Sitonik smiled and took off his necklace and put it over Supeet's head. He said something else, then turned and started back toward the kraal.

"Wait a second," I said.

Sitonik stopped and turned. I reached into my pocket and took out the kachina and held it out to him. He smiled broadly and took it from me. I didn't think Taw would mind. Sitonik said something. I turned to Supeet for a translation.

"He says that the kachina will be with you no matter where it lives."

With tears still flowing, Supeet watched the old

man disappear into the kraal. "We will go now," he said.

"What . . ."

"I will tell you soon," he interrupted. "Come." He put the leopard-skin bag under his shuka, and we walked away from the kraal.

As we headed east toward the Nguruman Escarpment, Supeet and I didn't talk. I knew that something very important had happened between him and Sitonik, but I didn't ask him what it was. I knew he would tell me when the time was right.

As we walked I thought about Supeet, my father, and Africa. I had more questions than answers, and for the first time in my life I realized that the questions might be more important than the answers. I felt more comfortable walking with Supeet than I did sitting in my living room in New York City. Perhaps Africa was my real home—something I knew my father had already discovered.

I saw things very differently now. It was as if I was in tune with the land around me. I was able to be myself, and I felt more alive than I ever had before. I was no longer a visitor. I was part of what was going on around me.

My mother said that mankind originated in Africa. In fact the oldest fossil remains of man had been found in northern Kenya. Perhaps I *was* home—the place where human history began.

We reached the riverbed by early afternoon and began following it south.

Breaking the long silence, Supeet said, "Sitonik is going to die."

I stopped and looked at him. "How do you know?"

"He told me," he said. "And a man like Sitonik knows when he is going to pass on."

I believed him. After all those years of life, Sitonik would definitely know when death was near. It made me very sad.

"He will be buried as a Laibon," Supeet continued. "When a Masai passes Sitonik's grave he will place a stone there in honor of him. Eventually a small hill of stones will mark his grave."

For some reason this custom sounded familiar to me, and I wondered if I had read about it in one of the books about Africa.

"Why did he give you the bag and the necklace?"

Supeet didn't answer right away, and we started walking again.

After a while he said, "I, too, am a Laibon."

I wasn't surprised by this. It explained a great deal about what had happened during the past few days—especially at the riverbed when he apparently knew I was floating above him.

"Then you are to take Sitonik's place?"

"Perhaps," he said. "Although no one can truly take another's place. With the necklace and the bones, Sitonik gave me some of his power and authority, but I may never have his knowledge. True power is held by knowledge, not by position."

"And he told you where to go to perform the rain ceremony?"

"Yes."

"Where is it?"

"Not far from here," he said. "And, oddly enough, *you* have seen it."

"What?"

"It is in the same cave you saw when you were outside your body."

He looked at me for a few moments, letting this sink in. I thought about the cave. I could see it clearly, and it wasn't my imagination or a dream. It was real. And I knew then that I had actually been there—that I had actually left my body. It was not a hallucination.

"What does all this mean, Supeet?"

"The cave is very old and sacred," he said. "Very few have been there. It is said that even to look in its direction can bring bad luck."

"But I was there!" I said.

Supeet laughed. "Your spirit was at the cave," he said. "And you were taken there—you had no choice. I think your luck will be good."

"Sitonik said I was going to have a difficult journey."

"The journeys of all young men are difficult."

"What about the ceremony?" I asked. "You don't have a drum."

"The rain drum is in the cave. It has only been used a few times. Sitonik has used it twice."

"And it worked?"

"Yes, Nkokua came."

"Nkokua?"

"The long rains."

"When will you perform the rain ceremony?"

"The moon will be full in two days."

PART III
Thunder Cave

I came to a sudden stop above a giant baobab tree. Below the tree was a huge pile of rocks. About a mile away from the tree was a cliff. I floated toward it. Along the cliff was a wide, steep path that led up to a cave opening. Ancient petroglyphs were painted on the wall outside the cave. I was wondering why I had been brought to this spot when I saw that one of the petroglyphs was the same snake design as Taw's amulet—a snake eating its tail.

Eighteen

By late afternoon we reached a crude road that ran along the Nguruman Escarpment.

"What do we do now?" I asked.

"We will look for your father's camp."

"What about the cave?"

"The cave is very near," Supeet said. "And the moon isn't full, so there is time."

I looked around. To our right was a steep hill. I pointed to it. "We might be able to see something from up there."

Supeet nodded, and we started up the hill. It was a difficult climb, but the view was worth it. On top, we could see for miles. The escarpment ran along the eastern base of the Lebetero Hills, which were at least twenty-five miles long. On the map they hadn't looked this big.

"There!" Supeet pointed.

A plume of dust rose in the distance, and it was a few moments before I could tell what was causing it.

"It's a truck!" I said excitedly. "Maybe it's my father, or maybe they know where he is." I started down the hill but Supeet grabbed my arm and jerked me back.

"Wait," he said.

"Why?" I was irritated. "I need to get to the road. They won't see us up here, and they'll drive right by."

"Just wait," Supeet insisted. "It will take no time to get to the bottom of the hill."

I didn't want to wait, but I did as he asked. We watched as the truck slowed to a stop and two men jumped out of the back and walked to the front of the truck.

"Poachers," Supeet said. "The same men from before. The same truck."

His eyesight must have been a lot better than mine. "How can you tell?"

"Look!" He pointed down to the left.

About a half mile away a small herd of elephants stood in a grove of trees.

"They are after the elephants," Supeet said. "The elephants have been running for a long time, but they are tired now. That's why they are bunched together in those trees."

I looked back at the truck. It moved about a hundred yards up the road, then stopped. The two men got out again and looked for elephant signs in the dust.

I had to stop them! My rage returned. I wouldn't stand by and watch them butcher more elephants. Before Supeet could stop me I began bounding down the steep hillside.

"No, Jacob!" he yelled after me.

But I didn't stop. I couldn't stop. When I got to the bottom I looked to my right and saw the truck racing up the road. I glanced back up the hill and saw Supeet coming down after me. I didn't wait for him. I ran across the road toward the elephants. When I was fifty yards away I started to wave my hands and yell as loud as I could. The elephants began to trumpet and move around nervously. I scooped up a rock and threw it at the rump of the nearest elephant. It swung around and flared its ears, but when the elephant saw me still running toward it, it turned and ran away. The rest of the herd followed.

I stopped and put my hands on my knees, trying to catch my breath as I watched the elephants stampede away. I didn't know if they'd get away from the poachers, but at least I had delayed another pointless slaughter. I turned, expecting to see an angry Supeet running up behind me. Instead I saw the poachers' truck bounce off the road and head directly toward the grove of trees.

I ran further into the grove, frantically looking for a place to hide, hoping they hadn't seen me. Then I heard rapid gunfire and saw tree bark splintering all around me. Wrong again, Jake. I froze, then very, very slowly turned around. Two men with rifles ran up and grabbed me roughly by my arms.

"Get your hands off me!" I tried to twist out of their grasp, but it was no use. They dragged me to the truck and pushed me up against the tailgate.

"I'm an American," I yelled. "And you better . . ."

Boom! One of the men hit me in the stomach with the butt of his rifle. I doubled over in agony and dropped to my knees. As I tried to regain my breath, I heard the truck doors slam. Four poachers—the same number as before. They spoke to each other in what sounded like Swahili. One of them started laughing and was joined by the other three. I recognized the cruel sound; Supeet was right, again. They were the same poachers. And where was Supeet? Too smart to take on four poachers. You idiot! Haven't you been

here before, Jake? Nairobi, wasn't it? Yeah, that's it—
the dark street. Three of them that time. I had a very
bad feeling that the guys in the street were angels compared to these guys.

I looked up at them. They had beards and wore
relatively new camouflage fatigues. The tallest man
wore a black beret, and I heard one of the men call
him Moja. He held a cocked automatic pistol in his
hand. When he stopped laughing, so did the other
men. I figured that he was their leader.

He looked down at me. "You are very stupid," he
said in passable English.

You're right about that, I thought.

"We know you are an American," he continued.
"But before I kill you, what is your name?"

Kill me? Why would he kill me? All I'd done was
chase a few elephants away. I wasn't going to give him
my name if it meant he would pull the trigger as soon
as he heard it.

"What are you doing here?"

"I didn't want you to get those elephants," I said.

"We saw what you did, but that does not answer
my question. Why are you out here?"

"I'm . . ." I hesitated.

"Why are you here?" he yelled, and put the pistol
barrel next to my head.

"I'm looking for my father," I said quickly.

"Who is your father?" He emphasized the question by pushing the barrel harder against my skull.

My mouth was bone dry, and I could barely get
the words out. "Robert Lansa," I whispered.

"Who?" he yelled.

"Dr. Robert Lansa," I said more loudly.

"Lansa," he said, taking the barrel away from my head. "We know Lansa. Does he know you're here?"

"Of course," I said.

"Stand up," he yelled.

I grabbed the tailgate and pulled myself up.

"Why are you so far from his camp?" he asked.

So they knew where he was! "I'm on my way to his camp," I said.

"I see." He put his pistol back in its holster.

There are no words for how relieved I was to see him do this. He turned to his men and said something. Two of them ran off toward the road.

He turned back to me. "It seems your friend has run off and left you." He looked at the road. "But we'll find him."

Not unless he wants to be found, I thought.

"Who is he?" he asked.

"Just a Masai I ran into," I said.

"A friend of yours?"

"No," I said. "Just a guy."

"I think not," he said. "What were you doing together?"

"Just traveling in the same direction," I said.

The poacher slapped me across the face, and I fell to the ground.

He looked down at me. "That was for lying," he said. "We will take you with us to kill the elephants." He kicked me in the stomach, knocking me halfway under the truck. I threw up. He waited for me to stop retching, then said, "That was for getting in our way. Don't do it again."

Bastard, I thought. Lousy bastard! I would rather die than see the elephants killed. It was bad enough to see it from a distance. Being right there would be horrible. The other poachers ran up to the truck. Supeet wasn't with them. I knew they wouldn't find him. At least my stupidity wasn't going to get him killed, too. I moved my head and felt something sharp prick my ear. I jerked away and turned and saw a large clump of razor-sharp thorns. A drop of blood dripped off my ear and spattered in the dust. What next? I thought disgustedly. Then an idea occurred to me. I looked out from under the truck. The poachers were still standing there talking, paying no attention to me.

I took hold of the thorn clump and very carefully and quietly pushed it in front of the rear truck wheel. My skin punctured easier than the tire, but it was worth a try. As soon as I had the thorns in place, one of the poachers grabbed me by the ankles and pulled me out from under the truck.

"Get in the truck!" Moja said. "Your elephants have not gone far."

I climbed into the bed among a pile of elephant tusks. He said something to the others, and two of them jumped into the bed with me. They pushed me toward the front and tied my wrists to the roll bar over the cab.

They started the truck and, with two armed poachers flanking me, we headed in the direction of the elephants. I waited for the sound of a blowout, but nothing happened. I was very disappointed. We cut through the grove and on the other side broke out onto an open savanna. I didn't see the elephants, but I knew they probably weren't too far away.

It was difficult to keep my feet under me as the truck gathered speed. After about a mile the truck leaned to the right and swerved. At first I thought the driver was trying to avoid a hole or something, but he slowed down and stopped. One of the poachers went to the back of the truck and looked over the side. He yelled something to Moja, who had stuck his head out the window.

They were mad as hell about the flat tire. I couldn't have been more pleased, but I didn't show it. They left me tied to the roll bar as they tried to get the tire changed. They were much better with their rifles than they were with a lug wrench and jack. I took great satisfaction in listening to them yell at each other. The longer they took the farther away the elephants would be.

When they were finished, Moja came around to the front of the truck and looked at the darkening sky. He said something to his men, and the two poachers jumped into the back.

"What are you going to do with me?" I asked.

Instead of answering he got into the cab and slammed the door. The driver started the truck and turned it around. They might kill me, but at least I wouldn't have to see any more elephants slaughtered.

We drove back the way we came, reaching the road along the escarpment just as the sun set behind the Lebetero Hills. I kept a sharp eye out for Supeet, but I didn't see a sign of him. There wasn't anything he could do anyway. And he had more important things to do than to try to save the stupid American kid he had befriended. I was on my own.

At the road the truck turned left and headed south. To the side of the road I saw animal eyes illuminated by the truck's headlights. We drove for several miles down the dusty road, then came to an abrupt stop in front of an impala momentarily blinded by our headlights. It stood frozen in the middle of the road. The driver turned the truck's spotlight on, and the poacher to my right raised his rifle and shot. The impala dropped where it was standing. The other poacher slapped his friend on the back. They jumped out, picked up the impala, and carried it back to the truck. The poachers climbed in, took up their positions next to me, and the truck lurched off again.

I figured that the impala was dinner and that wherever we were going was close by or they would have cut the impala's throat and bled it out. I was right. A short time later, the truck stopped and took a sharp right turn, leaving the road. We went up a very steep grade in low gear. In front of us I saw the lights of several campfires and lanterns hanging from trees. At least a dozen men were in the camp, perhaps more. Some of them were sitting by the fires cooking, while others were bent over stretched animal skins, scraping the fat off with knives.

The truck pulled up to several other trucks and jeeps and stopped. Everyone got out except for me. Moja strode to the middle of the camp and called out. Two young Masai warriors, armed with spears, ran up to him. He gestured toward the truck as he spoke to them. They nodded and ran over to untie me, then led me to Moja.

"Welcome to our little camp," he said.

I looked around me. It was a nightmare. Scattered throughout the camp were huge piles of elephant tusks. Animal skins hung from every branch, and the place reeked with the stink of death. I could hear the incessant buzzing of flies above the sound of the men's voices and laughter.

"I can see you like it here," the poacher said, and laughed. "We will feed you and give you water so you do not think that we are totally uncivilized." He laughed again and said something to one of the Masai, who ran off. In a moment the Masai ran back with a canteen of water and handed it to me. I took a long drink, wishing that I had a little of Supeet's powder. But since they were going to kill me, what difference did it make?

"What are you going to do with me?"

The poacher looked at me. "You are going to die," he said. "But first I want you to see us kill your elephant friends."

"Why don't you just kill me now?" I said. Being at his mercy didn't mean I had to take his crap.

He slapped me, but I didn't fall down this time.

"Because it doesn't please me to kill you now!" He glared at me. "And you may be useful. We shall see."

"What do you mean by that?"

He ignored the question and said something to the warriors. They took me over to a tree at the edge of the camp, made me sit down, then tied me to it. The warriors took up positions ten feet away on either side of me and leaned on their spears. Why would they go to all of this trouble only to kill me? I looked at the men, now unloading the ivory from the truck. They were a rough-looking bunch.

I couldn't brush the flies away and had to shake my head from time to time to get them off my face. I watched the men and looked at the carnage. It was a wonder that there were any animals left in Africa.

After a while Moja came over to me with a hunk of meat from the fire. He told one of the Masai to untie me and handed me the meat. He watched as I forced myself to eat but said nothing to me.

When I finished eating, Moja ordered the Masai to tie me back up.

Nineteen

The fires burned down and the lanterns were put out, throwing the camp into semidarkness. One by one the men wandered off to sleep, leaving only the sound of flies buzzing and men snoring. The two Masai stood like statues on either side of me, looking straight ahead. I tried to loosen the ropes with my numb arms, but it was hopeless.

I wondered if Supeet had found the cave. I tapped out the cadence of Sitonik's drumbeat with my foot. I wondered if I would ever see Supeet again. If it rained before I died I'd know that he had made it. I'd been given a second chance at life, but I had wasted it by being rash. *"Your dad's pretty damn stubborn!"* Like father like son, I thought.

My chin kept dropping to my chest. Each time this happened I snapped my head back up and forced my eyes open. I was determined to stay awake until the end. I had very little time, and I wasn't going to spend it sleeping.

As the night wore on I dozed more often, and my chin stayed on my chest for longer periods. *Wake up, Jake! Wake up!* I snapped my head up and tried to shake the sleep away. I looked around through blurry eyes and thought that I saw something, or someone, move on the other side of the camp, but when I blinked and looked again, I saw nothing. My chin dropped to my chest again.

The next time I lifted my head I saw Supeet standing in the dim light of the closest fire. I almost shouted but caught myself. I held my breath and, using just my eyes, glanced at the two Masai on either side of me. To my amazement they had not changed positions. Their eyes were wide open, staring straight ahead at Supeet, but they couldn't see him because he had camouflaged his body.

Supeet stood frozen with one foot poised above the ground. He held his spear horizontally in his right hand, straight out from his side. If I could see him, why couldn't they? It wasn't possible. Then I realized what was happening. The guards were standing ten feet away on either side of me. Their eyes were four feet above mine, and they saw what I saw at a slightly different angle. I could see a small part of the spear shaft, but from where the Masai stood they must have seen only the tip of the spear point, which was like looking straight at the edge of a razor blade. In other words, they couldn't see the spear at all. As Supeet made his approach, he wasn't thinking about what he was seeing, he was thinking about what the Masai were seeing—in his mind he stood with them, watching himself approach and moving accordingly. He used the shadows and background to camouflage himself perfectly. In effect, he *was* invisible.

Enthralled, I watched as he inched his way toward us. The only way I knew he was actually moving was to recall his last position. Why he had decided to come at us straight on rather than from behind I didn't know. Perhaps he thought the effect would be much greater if he appeared in front of the young warriors suddenly. It took him a long while to work his way forward, and I began to worry about the time. Supeet was incredible, but he'd never be able to do this in daylight.

When he was ten feet away he stood perfectly still. I watched his rib cage. He barely breathed. The warriors continued to look straight ahead, totally oblivious to his presence. Finally, he took a regular step forward and swung his spear in front of him. I looked at the morans. They stood with their mouths open, flabbergasted, too shocked to speak. To them it must have looked like Supeet appeared from out of thin air. The Masai to my right very carefully and quietly placed his spear on the ground. The other Masai looked at him and did the same. Supeet motioned for them to step forward. They hesitated, then walked up to him and bowed their heads. Supeet leaned forward and whispered something to them. They nodded, picked up their spears, and quietly walked out of the camp.

Supeet grinned and walked over to me. I was about to say something, but he motioned for me to be quiet by putting his finger to his lips. He squatted next to me and cut the ropes with his knife. I had trouble moving my arms.

He leaned close to my ear and whispered, "Like I taught you."

I knew what he meant. I pulled my tennis shoes off.

We walked out of the camp very slowly, but not nearly as slowly as Supeet had come into it. When we got to the trucks, Supeet retrieved his shuka and quickly put it on.

Just as we were leaving the camp an armed poacher suddenly stepped in front of us. He was momentarily confused. Before he could figure out what was happening, Supeet swung his spear and knocked the rifle from his hand. The man dove for the rifle, but when he turned around with it, Supeet ran the blade of his spear into his chest. The man screamed, but the sound died quickly. I stood in shock, looking at the blood pumping out of the open wound.

"Come," Supeet said urgently, pulling me.

The man's scream had awakened the camp, and the still night was shattered by shouts of alarm.

"We must go!" Supeet said. "There is a time to move slowly and a time to move quickly." He began to run down the steep path and I followed.

By the time we reached the escarpment road I heard the engines of the poachers' trucks. I glanced back up the hill and saw several spotlights cutting through the dark night.

We started running east through the open bush. The moon was nearly full, making it relatively easy to avoid bushes and trees. I looked back and saw that the trucks and jeeps had reached the escarpment road. Some of them turned right, some turned left, and others headed overland directly toward us. There was no way we'd be able to outrun them.

"We must keep going," Supeet said. "I know a good place to hide. At least for a little while."

He led me to a large kopje. "Climb," he said.

We scrambled up and between huge boulders. At the top Supeet said, "This way!"

I followed him over to the narrow crevice between

two boulders. He squeezed through, and I was right behind him. Once through the opening, the space got bigger.

We both leaned against the cool rocks and caught our breath. There was just enough moonlight shining in to illuminate us. For the third time, Supeet had saved my life. It was like he was my guardian angel or something. And I was keeping him a lot busier than I wanted to.

"I shouldn't have gone after the elephants," I said.

He looked at me. "No," he said. "That was a mistake."

"It's just that I didn't want to see the elephants get killed. I couldn't stand by without doing anything."

"You did what you felt you had to do," he said. "You cannot make good decisions without making bad decisions. Life is made of opposites. The next time you try to save the elephants you will do it more effectively, although I noticed that the elephants *did* get away."

"You were there?"

"Close enough to see," he said. "Was the flat tire a coincidence?"

"No," I said, and told him about the thorns.

He smiled and sat down on the ground.

For the first time since I'd met him he looked tired. The stalk and run must have taken everything out of him.

"Why did the warriors walk away?"

"They left out of fear and respect. My sudden appearance frightened them, and because I wear this necklace, they thought I was Sitonik."

"What did you tell them?"

"I told them to go back to the cattle and the people and to never work for the poachers again."

I heard a truck pull up and stop near the kopje. A beam of light swept past our hiding place, then the truck drove away.

"We will wait here until they come back past us," Supeet said. "Then we will leave. In the morning they may send trackers out looking for you. In the daylight it will not take them long to find this place."

"I don't think they'll waste their time," I said. "The only reason they didn't kill me right away was so I could see the elephants slaughtered."

"You underestimate them," Supeet said. "They are very clever men, and I don't think they kept you alive to see the elephants die. Evil is smart—never forget this. You were spared for a reason, but I don't know what it is. I am going to sleep for now," he said. "When the truck passes again, wake me, and we will leave."

I wanted to ask him where we were going to go, but he was already starting to lie down. He was halfway to the ground when he froze. At first I didn't know what was happening. I followed his gaze and saw the dim outline of a very large snake. The snake raised its head and stopped just inches from Supeet's face, then spread its enormous hood—a cobra! The snake hissed loudly and shot a glob of something into Supeet's face. Yelling in agony, Supeet rolled to the side. Without thinking, I grabbed his spear and swung it at the snake. The spear's sharp blade sliced through its body easily and the two parts writhed for a few moments before lying still.

Supeet held his face in his hands.

"What is it, Supeet," I yelled. "What can I do?"

"A cobra," he said in anguish. "A spitting cobra. My eyes. Stay away from it."

"I killed it!" I said, putting my arms around him. "What can I do?"

Through clenched teeth he said, "Pour water into my eyes!"

Hurriedly I grabbed the water gourd and removed the stopper. I put his head in my lap. "I'm ready," I said.

He took his hands away from his face and with great difficulty opened his eyes and kept them open as I poured the water.

"That's enough," he said, closing his eyes and sitting up. "Let me have your shirt."

I pulled it off and he carefully wiped his eyes with it. When he was finished he handed it back to me and sat there for a few moments, then turned to me.

"Pour more water."

I did as he asked.

He blinked his eyes and said, "I am blind."

"Blind?" I couldn't believe it. "I have to get you to a hospital," I said.

Supeet smiled grimly. "We are a long way from a hospital, Jake. The blindness may not last; it depends on the amount of damage. I will know in a few days, and it would take that long to get to a hospital."

"What are we going to do?"

"We will wait until the poachers head back to their camp and then you will leave."

"What do you mean *I* will leave? What about *you?*"

"You must escape," he said. "I will only slow you down. Find your father. I will be fine here."

"I'm not leaving you here."

"You must!"

"Like hell!" There was no way that I was going to leave him on this kopje. "What about the cave and the rain ceremony?"

He was silent for a few moments. "I'm afraid," he said sadly, "that I will miss the full moon. Perhaps another time."

"Sitonik said that it has to happen during this full moon, and I'm going to get you to that cave!"

"But your father—"

"My father doesn't even know I'm here," I said. "When we first met you said that I might be here for another reason besides finding my father. I know what that reason is now."

"It will be difficult with a blind man."

"You said that the journeys of all young men are difficult!"

Supeet smiled. "I think I'll rest now," he said. "Do you see any more snakes?"

I hadn't even thought about other snakes. Some guardian angel I'd make. I took his spear and poked around in some of the darker areas. "I think it's clear."

"Good," he said, lying down. "Wake me before it's light."

Twenty

I waited until Supeet was asleep, then slipped out through the crevice and climbed to the top of the kopje. In the distance I saw the headlights of a poacher's truck heading away from us back toward the camp. To the east the sky was beginning to lighten. Supeet wanted to leave while it was still dark in order to get a head start on the poachers. But I was almost certain they'd call off the search—they were more interested in elephants than they were in me. I wanted to give Supeet more time to rest, so I sat on top of the boulder a little longer.

After what I'd seen Supeet do in the camp, I had no doubt that he could make it rain whether he was blind or sighted. If it wasn't for me Supeet would have already been at the cave.

I climbed down the boulder and squeezed through the opening. Supeet was still asleep. I gently shook him.

"We've got to go," I whispered. "The poachers are gone."

He sat up slowly. "Are you sure?"

"I saw them driving back to camp."

"Good."

"How do you want to do this?" I asked.

He thought for a moment. "I should be able to tell where you are by listening," he said. "But out in the open I will put my hand on your shoulder, and you can guide me."

"How do I find the cave?"

"You will have to tell me what you see," he said. "And I will guide *you*. First, go back to the escarpment road."

We left the hiding place and very carefully climbed down the kopje. At the bottom we headed west across the open bush toward the road. Supeet had his hand on my shoulder and adjusted his pace to mine. I promised myself that no matter what happened I would get him to the cave safely. The long rains were more important than finding my father.

When we reached the escarpment road I stopped. "Which way?"

"South." He raised his face toward the sky. "I feel the sun."

"It's just coming up." Both of his eyes were badly swollen.

As we followed the road south I told him what I was seeing. Periodically I glanced behind, looking for dust from the poachers' trucks. I still didn't believe that they'd come after us, but I kept my eyes open for places we could hide just in case.

"Soon we will come to a dry streambed coming down from the hills," Supeet said. "From there we turn west and follow the stream up into the hills."

About a mile later I saw it. "The streambed is just ahead." I led him over to it, and we started the climb.

"On the other side of this hill will be a narrow valley."

When we got to the top I saw it. The flat savanna valley was only a few hundred yards wide. On the other side was another hill, roughly the same height as the hill we were standing on. Both hills were covered with thick brush and trees. I told Supeet what I saw.

"Good. Take me down into the valley."

It was difficult walking down the steep brushy hillside, and we were both grateful when we reached the valley floor.

"Walk north," Supeet said. "Until you see a large grove of yellow-fever trees on the right."

I led him along the base of the west hill until I saw the grove.

"We're at the grove," I said.

"Take me through it."

We walked through the grove, and when we came through the other side I knew where we were. It was the same place I'd seen in my dream. In front of us stood a gigantic baobab tree surrounded by a huge pile of stones. I noticed something I hadn't noticed in the dream—the grass around the stones was green as if it had been regularly watered. I hadn't seen green grass since I left New York.

"I know where the cave is," I said.

"Then you see the baobab?"

"It's hard to miss," I said, and added quietly, "and I've been here before."

Supeet smiled, and said, "Take me to the baobab."

When we got there Supeet kneeled and felt the stones. "This is where Lumeya is buried," he said.

"Lumeya?"

Supeet sat down. "A great man," he said. "When he was a small boy a Masai warrior found him alone in the bush. The only thing he had with him was a magical box called Enkidong. The warrior took him back to his family, and they discovered that he could foretell the future and that he knew of a secret water place. He became the first Laibon of the Masai, and the Enkidong has been passed down to each Laibon in his line."

I looked down at the green grass. "Is this where Lumeya found water?"

Supeet felt the grass and smiled. "It could be," he said. "But in the story the place isn't specified."

"How long has he been buried here?"

"How many stones do you see?"

I looked around. "Hundreds—maybe more."

"Well," Supeet said. "The only person allowed to place a stone on Lumeya's grave is another Laibon, and very few of them have ever been here."

"In other words," I said, "Lumeya has been here a very long time."

Supeet nodded.

"What happened to the magical box?" I asked.

"Sitonik destroyed it."

"What?" I couldn't believe it. "Why would he do that?"

Supeet laughed. "He said he got tired of carrying it around with him, so he took the contents and made this necklace and the rest he put into a small pouch."

"You mean the bones and the necklace are Lumeya's magic Enkidong?"

"Correct."

"What kind of magic?"

"I will spend the rest of my life finding that out." Supeet stood up. "I need your help."

"Anything," I said.

173

He reached out and felt my shoulders, then dropped to his knees in front of me. He then drew his knife from the sheath beneath his shuka and handed it to me.

"I need you to shave my head, he said. "Use a little water and try not to cut me—go slowly."

I took the gourd from his shoulder and poured a small amount of water over his head and very carefully began scraping his hair off. When I was finished I dried his head with my T-shirt.

He raised his head. "How does it look?"

"Slick," I said.

He laughed. "Good. Now go to the green grass and dig until you reach mud and bring a handful to me."

I dug under the soft grass and in no time reached moist reddish clay. I scooped out a double handful and watched as water filled the hole where the mud had been. Water won't be a problem here, I thought. Then I realized that there was something strange about this place. *Look at the white space, Jake. Sometimes it's the things we can't see and don't hear that are the most important.* I looked around. The place was like an oasis in the middle of a desert. It should have been swarming with animals, but I didn't see or hear a single one.

I brought the mud over to where Supeet was sitting. "There are no animals here," I said.

"I know," Supeet said. "I wondered how long it would take you to notice. Sitonik said that only special animals come here."

"Why? There's water, green grass . . ."

"He didn't say."

"What did he mean by *special* animals?"

"I don't know."

I looked around again and felt very uncomfortable. When I came to Africa I was nervous about encountering animals in the wild; now I was uneasy about not encountering them. What kind of place was this?

"Do you have the mud?"

"Yes," I said, still holding it in my cupped hands.

"Good. I want you to put a thin coat on my head, face, and neck."

I knelt in front of him and began to smear mud on his shaved head and worked my way down. When I got to his eyelids, I hesitated. They were still badly swollen, and I didn't want to hurt him.

"On the eyes, too," Supeet said.

I continued spreading the mud on his eyelids very, very gently. He winced in pain and I stopped.

"I can't, Supeet!"

"You must," he said. "You're doing fine."

I continued, but I wasn't very happy about it. I took a step back and looked at my handiwork.

"How does it look?"

"Very handsome," I said.

"Thank you," he said. "Now, find a stone for me to put on the pile."

I jogged over to the yellow-fever trees, found a stone, and brought it back. Supeet held the stone in both hands and said a few words, then very gently placed it on the pile. As soon as he removed his hand, he fell over backward and his body began to shake violently.

I rushed over and put my arms around him, trying to help. The convulsions grew worse and shook my entire body, then stopped as suddenly as they had begun.

"What happened?" I asked. "Are you all right?"

"I'm fine," he said, sitting up slowly. He felt the stones on Lumeya's grave. "Sitonik has died."

"Oh . . . ," I said, feeling the grief I'd felt when my mother died welling up inside me. "I don't know what to say, Supeet. I'm very sorry."

Tears spilled from his swollen eyes. "He will be missed."

Supeet sat for several minutes with his head bowed, then got to his feet. "Please take me to the cave," he said quietly. "It is time."

I stood, and he put his hand on my shoulder. We walked past the baobab to the beginning of the path.

"We're at the path leading to the cave," I said. "It's very steep." It was also wide—a good ten feet across. And it was well worn, as if it were heavily traveled. I wondered who had made it.

Supeet put his hand on my shoulder, and we started up. It didn't take me long to figure out why the path was so worn. Elephant dung was strewn all over it, and some of the piles looked relatively fresh.

"I'd say elephants use this path pretty regularly."

"Africa's perfect path builders," Supeet said. "They are fueled by grass, know the easiest way between two points, manufacture their own replacements, and live for a long time."

All good points, I thought. But I was more interested in why they hadn't turned the grass around the baobab into a mud wallow. I asked Supeet what he thought about this.

"Perhaps Lumeya keeps them away," he said. "It is said that he was buried standing up so he could continue to see all around him."

"Do you think there are elephants in the cave?" I asked.

"We'll know soon," he said.

A couple of minutes later we stood outside the cave entrance. I looked at the petroglyphs on the outside wall. Aside from the snake eating its tail, there were many others. One depicted a group of warriors hunting a herd of animals. Another looked like clouds with giant black thunderbolts coming out of them.

A cool damp breeze came from the opening, and with it the unmistakable musky odor of elephants. The entrance was more than large enough for an elephant to pass through.

I peered into the darkness but could only see about ten feet inside. "I don't see any elephants," I said.

"And I don't hear any," Supeet said. "Shall we go in?"

"I guess." ·

Once inside I stood for a few moments, letting my eyes adjust to the darkness. It was cold. I felt like I had just stepped into an air-conditioned warehouse. I heard the echo of trickling water and was surprised to see a good-size pool in the center of the cave. This could explain why the elephants hadn't turned Lumeya's grave into a wallow, but it didn't explain why there weren't hundreds of animals around here.

Supeet took a deep breath and said, "Salt."

"What?"

"The cave has salt in it." He reached down and scooped up a handful of reddish dirt and tasted it. I did the same. He was right. "The elephants come here for the salt. Perhaps it is their reward for maintaining the path. What do you see?"

I looked up. The ceiling was at least forty feet above us. "It's huge," I said.

"There should be a small passage."

I looked around and saw darker areas that had to be tunnels, but from where I was I couldn't tell how deep they were. "There are several," I said.

"One of them should have a light coming from it."

I strained my eyes to see and thought I saw a small amount of light coming from a tunnel on the wall in front of us. As we walked toward it, the light grew brighter. We stopped outside the opening and I looked down the narrow passage.

"This must be it," I said. "But it's going to be a tight fit. We'll have to crawl. I'll go first and check it out."

I slid into the tunnel and wormed my way down the long passage. The tunnel led to a good-size cavern that, surprisingly, was as cold as a refrigerator. Water trickled down the far wall, spilling into another pool of water, much smaller than the pool in the main cave. The light came from an opening in the top of the ceiling. The walls around the cavern were decorated with hundreds of ancient petroglyphs depicting animals and people. Above them were billowing clouds with rain falling from them.

I yelled down the tunnel that I thought this must be the place. There was a delay, and I heard, *"This is the place, Supeet! This is the place, Supeet! This is the place, Su. . . ."* My voice was duplicated perfectly; it was weird to hear it bouncing off the walls.

A few moments later Supeet emerged from the tunnel. I told him about the petroglyphs on the walls and the light coming from the ceiling.

"Lead me directly under the light," he said. I did as he asked, and he sat down.

"There is a drum on the wall," he said.

I walked over to the wall. Sitting on a narrow ledge was a very old drum much like the one Sitonik had used in the hut. When I picked it up, I heard something *plunk* inside. I shook it. "There's something inside," I said.

"Lumeya's first wife," Supeet said.

"What?"

"Well, not his whole wife," he said. "Just her skull."

"You've got to be kidding!" I shook it again.

"That's what Sitonik told me. He said that Lumeya's first wife was . . . how shall I put it? She was very severe. She sometimes beat him with a stick, so when she died he had her skull put into his favorite drum."

What goes around comes around, I thought. "How was his other wife?"

"He had several. Apparently the others were all right."

I took the drum over and handed it to him.

"What now?"

Supeet held the drum between his crossed legs. "We need a fire."

He was right about that; I was shivering. I'd have to haul in wood from outside, and it wasn't going to be easy to get the wood down the narrow tunnel.

"How long will we be here?" I asked.

"Until the long rains come."

What if they don't come? I thought. What if it takes weeks or months? I pictured myself bringing wood and food to him indefinitely.

"I'll start bringing wood in."

"Jacob?"

I stopped and turned.

"I could not have done this on my own," he said. "Thank you."

"If it hadn't been for me," I said, "you'd still have your sight."

"I think not," he said. "The snake was waiting for me. If it wasn't at the kopje, it would have been waiting somewhere else. Sitonik told me you would guide me. I didn't understand what he meant until the snake took my sight."

Twenty-one

By that evening I had a nice fire going, and the cavern was warm. Supeet sat cross-legged in front of the fire, chanting and pounding the drum. Earlier in the day he had fallen into a trance, and he no longer answered when I asked him something. His chanting echoed through the cavern and sounded like a choir in a cathedral. He occupied the same space as me, but he was clearly someplace else.

I sat down across from him. I'd gathered plenty of wood, but the dried meat that we had gotten at Sitonik's kraal was nearly gone. I was going to have to do something about this, but it would have to wait till morning. Exhausted, I lay down and fell asleep.

Twice during the night I woke. Supeet continued to chant, and as far as I could tell he hadn't changed positions. I didn't know how he kept it up.

The third time I woke, I saw light coming through the opening in the ceiling. I was famished, but I didn't eat. Supeet would need what little food we had when and if he came out of his trance. It was time for me to try my hand at borrowing food.

I put several more pieces of wood on the fire and stacked a small pile right next to Supeet. If the borrowing took longer than I expected, I hoped he'd be able to come out of his trance long enough to stoke the fire.

I looked around the cavern one more time, making

sure that everything was all right. Supeet continued to chant and beat the drum. I walked over and watched him for a moment. I took the amulet from around my neck and gently put it over his head, figuring that he needed it more than I did. I then took his spear and water gourd and crawled through the narrow tunnel.

Outside the cave the bright sunlight burned my eyes. Another cloudless day. The view from the path was spectacular. I could see for miles. Beneath the cave was the narrow valley. Just over the top of the west hill I saw a few vultures circling. I figured that they might be soaring over something worth borrowing. It was several miles away, but it seemed like a good place to start.

I walked down the steep path past Lumeya's grave and the baobab. Twenty minutes later I reached the bottom of the hill and started across the valley. The only way to get to where the vultures were circling was to climb the west hill. It took me an hour to reach the top. The vultures were circling over a small group of trees near a kopje. I watched a vulture circle lower and lower, then land in one of the trees. I didn't know what they were eating, but at least I now knew where it was. I walked down the hill very slowly, hoping that the kill had not been made by lions. I didn't think my borrowing skills were ready for that. When I got to the bottom I stalked slowly toward the trees. There were several vultures perched on the branches. Under one of the trees a zebra lay on its side. From where I was I could hear its heavy breathing. It was obviously injured, but there were no predators in sight. Supeet hadn't covered this in his instructions on borrowing. There was supposed to be a cheetah, leopard, or hyena gnawing on the luckless prey. Where were they?

For a long time I stayed where I was, trying to decide the best way to approach the situation. I continually scanned the landscape for predators, but the only thing I saw were more and more vultures fluttering into the trees. I decided that I'd use the birds as my guide. They had a lot more experience at this than I did, and I was sure they wouldn't move in on the zebra until they thought it was safe. An hour passed. The vultures began dropping from the trees to the ground. The zebra's breathing was less audible, but I could see its sides still heaving. Finally I couldn't stand it anymore. I stood up and screamed as loud as I could and ran over to the trees, swinging the spear over my head. The vultures scattered. When I got to the zebra I turned completely around looking for predators, but didn't see any.

The zebra's eyes were wide open in terror. It tried to struggle, but it could hardly move its once powerful legs. It looked relatively young and healthy and there weren't any fang and claw marks on its neck or flank. What had brought it down? In a final attempt to get up, the zebra kicked with its hind legs, and then I saw the wire snare. Those bastards! They probably got no more than a few dollars for a zebra skin! I hadn't seen the wire at first because it was buried deeply into the zebra's leg. The snare was anchored around the tree, and every time the zebra kicked the noose tightened, digging the wire deeper into the flesh of its leg. I noticed now that the leg was terribly swollen. Only the vultures knew how long it had lain here suffering.

I thought about trying to get the wire off and letting the zebra up. But even if it could stand and walk, it wouldn't be able to run, and without this ability, its chances in the bush were zero.

I squatted near the zebra's head and stroked its muscular neck. "I'm sorry," I said. "It's the only way." I stood and raised the spear above my head and plunged the point into the zebra's chest cavity. Blood gushed from the wound, spilling onto the black-and-white hair. I raised the spear again and brought it down. The zebra stiffened, then went limp. Sickened, I turned away just in time to see a group of Grant's gazelles streak past behind me. What were they running from? I looked in the direction they had come from and saw a plume of dust. A second later a jeep came roaring into the clearing. I recognized it immediately. Poachers!

If I got caught, who would take care of Supeet? I started to run. I heard the explosion of gunfire, but I didn't stop. I ran to the kopje and scrambled up the side. Their jeep wouldn't be able to manage the grade. If they wanted me, they'd have to chase me on foot. I glanced back and saw the jeep stop and the men jump out. More gunfire. Bullets peppered the dirt and boulders around me, but I made it up and over the top, where I was temporarily safe. I stopped to catch my breath and looked back. The two men were climbing up after me. My best chance was to run down the other side of the kopje, then cut back toward the hill. It would take them a while to figure out which way I went. In order for them to catch me on the open savanna, they'd have to get back to their jeep. By that time I'd be on the hillside in a familiar area.

I looked in the direction of the cave. Above the east hill a single cloud had formed. I blinked and

looked again. It wasn't a hallucination. The rain ceremony must be working! I looked back down the kopje.
The men were still climbing after me.

I had to make a decision. The poachers may have
radioed for help. If I went back to the cave, they might
track me there and capture not only me but Supeet as
well. I couldn't take the chance. I took another look at
the cloud, still not believing it. If I was destined to get
caught it was going to be as far away from the cave as
I could lead them. My only hope now was to put as
much distance between me and them as I could. I
dashed down the other side of the kopje.

At the bottom I headed west away from the cave.
I was sure the two poachers would see me from the
top of the kopje, but I didn't have any choice. Three
miles away was another kopje. If I could reach it
before they caught up to me I might be able to find a
place to hide.

About halfway to the kopje I heard the sound of
an engine in the distance. My heart sank—I wasn't
going to make it. I turned, expecting to see the jeep
bearing down on me, but it wasn't there. The drone of
the engine grew louder and louder. Where was it coming from? I looked up. A small single-engine airplane
was above me. It waggled its wings back and forth in
greeting as it passed. Had my father fixed his airplane?
I watched it bank left. It cut its engines and came in
for a landing. I watched as the airplane gently touched
down on the dry savanna and came to a stop fifty feet
away from me.

The door opened and a man jumped out of the
plane. It wasn't my father. The man had gray hair
and a very dark tan and wore a khaki-colored safari

outfit. He smiled broadly at me. I hesitated. What was he doing out here? Cautiously I walked over to him.

"Damn," he said cheerfully. "You *are* white!"

"You're an American?" I asked suspiciously.

"Born and bred," he said. "What the hell are you doing out here?"

"It's a long story," I said. "Right now I'm running from some poachers."

"Poachers?"

I nodded.

"I saw those guys. They're on the other side of that kopje. You say they're after you?"

"Yeah."

"Well, unless they can fly they aren't going to catch you."

I started to feel a little better about him. "What are you doing out here?" I asked.

"I just bought this airplane from a friend," he said, proudly slapping the wing. "I was taking it for a joyride." He laughed. "I almost stalled the damn thing when I saw you. It isn't every day that you see a white boy with a spear running across the savanna. I figured you might need some help."

"You figured right," I said. "Do you live around here?"

"I do now. Retired about five years ago. Me and the wife moved from Pittsburgh to Narok. Big contrast, but we love it!"

I looked back toward the kopje—worried about the poachers. "The poachers aren't too happy with me. The last time I saw them they were shooting."

"No kidding?" A look of alarm crossed his face.

"Well, I don't want them to shoot up my plane. Do you want me to take you somewhere?"

Good question. If I had him take me back to the cave, the poachers might see us land, and they'd know where I was. I looked toward the cave. Supeet seemed to be doing fine without me. I'd go back to the cave when things cooled down.

"I'm trying to find my father," I said. "He's a field biologist, and his camp is supposed to be somewhere around here."

"What's his name?"

"Robert Lansa."

The man snapped his fingers. "I've heard of him. Elephant researcher, right?"

"That's right!"

"Never met him, but I hear about him all the time. Your old man's a pretty famous guy. My wife's a big fan of his. We support what he's trying to do for the elephants."

"Do you know where his camp is?"

"Not exactly," he said. "But I flew over a small camp earlier that could have been his. Let's go find out! If it isn't his camp, they might know where he is. Hop in!"

He climbed into the plane. "You can put the water gourd in back and the spear between the seats. Those are Masai, aren't they?"

I nodded.

"Wait until my wife hears about this. She was giving me a bad time about buying this plane, and the first day I have it, I save an American kid from poachers. She won't believe it! By the way, what's your name?"

"Jacob."

"Pleased to meet you, Jacob." He put his hand out, and we shook. "My name's Michael Donovan, but my friends call me Donny."

"Glad to meet you," I said. "And thanks!"

"Happy to be of service. Now let's get out of here."

He started the engine and pushed the throttle forward, bringing the plane around. He slipped a radio headset over his ears and shouted for me to do the same.

"Can you hear me?" he asked.

I nodded.

"Great! We're off!" He pushed the throttle forward, and the plane bounced over the savanna gathering speed. He pulled back on the stick, and we took off.

I was safe, and I might even see my father before the end of the day. It was hard to believe. If the poachers hadn't shown up I might not have come across Donny.

Donny leveled the airplane out and flew north toward the kopje where the poachers were. "We'll keep it at about two thousand feet. We should be able to see everything we need to see from that altitude. Looky here!" He pointed out his window and banked the plane to the right. The poachers' jeep was speeding across the savanna. I saw the kopje I'd been running toward and realized I would have never made it. The poachers stopped the jeep and watched us. I thought they might take a few potshots, but they didn't.

"If I had guns on this baby," Donny said angrily. "I'd blow them to hell." By the look on his face I didn't doubt that he would have.

"So I take it that your father doesn't know you're out here," he said.

"No," I said. "I wasn't able to reach him." I told him about my mother dying and how I had gotten to Africa.

"Well, you got guts," he said. "No doubt about it. Why were the poachers after you?"

"I was in the wrong place at the wrong time," I said.

Donny laughed. "Been there myself a few times. Say now, that's something different." He pointed out my side of the airplane. The cloud above the east hill had grown much larger and darker.

"Haven't seen clouds around here in a while," he said. "This drought has been a bad deal all the way around."

I didn't mention why I thought the cloud was there. I could hardly believe the reason myself.

"How far is the camp?" I asked.

"Not far as the crow flies. We'll be over it in a few minutes."

As we flew on I kept my eyes glued to the window, looking for the camp.

"How long has it been since you saw your dad?" he asked.

"A couple of years," I said, and thought, Way too long.

"He'll be surprised."

"You're not kidding!" And I wondered just what his reaction would be.

"There it is," Donny said. "Right near those trees."

I looked at the trees and saw a Land Rover parked next to a couple of tents and a small airplane. "I think it's my father's Land Rover!" I recognized it from the photos he'd sent.

Donny looked around to his right and left. "There isn't a good place to land around here," he said. "I'll try to raise him on the radio. See if we can arrange a place to meet." He reached for the microphone. "This is Cessna to camp. Cessna to camp. Does anybody copy?" He dipped the wing of the airplane and began to circle and keyed the mike again. "Does anybody copy down there?"

I saw a man come out from under the awning of a tent and look up. A second later he was joined by another man that looked like my father, but he was too far away for me to be sure. The second man walked over to the other tent.

"This is the camp, over." My father's voice! I'd traveled thousands of miles to see him, and I was now only a few hundred feet away.

Donny keyed the mike again. "Is this the camp of Dr. Robert Lansa?"

"Yes."

"Am I speaking to Dr. Lansa?"

"Yes."

Donny smiled at me and winked.

"Wonderful," Donny said. "Could you switch to channel twenty-nine?"

"Switching to two-niner," my father said.

I could hardly contain myself. I wanted to rip the mike out of Donny's hand.

Donny turned the radio dial to twenty-nine. "Are you there?"

"Roger," my father said. "Go ahead, over."

"Dr. Lansa, you don't know me, but I have sitting

next to me someone you haven't seen in a long time. He'd like to speak to you."

Donny held the mike in front of me. "Go ahead," he said. "Say hello to your dad." He keyed the mike.

"Dad!" I said. "It's me!"

"Jacob? What the hell? What are you doing . . ."

Donny took the mike away from my face and keyed it again. "Your son, Dr. Lansa. I found him wandering in the bush. It seems that there were some poachers after him."

"I don't believe this! How did Jacob—"

"Let's get down to business," Donny interrupted, the tone of his voice changing abruptly. He held the key down and continued. "We share a common interest, Dr. Lansa—an interest in elephants. I want you to listen very carefully. Tomorrow at dawn I want you to meet Jacob and me by the Nguruman Escarpment twenty kilometers from Kelema. I think you know the place. Do you copy?"

Dawn, I thought. There was plenty of light to land the plane this afternoon, and if I remembered the map right, Kelema was near the cave. Why would we have to fly all the way back there?

"What's going on?" my father asked. "What are you saying?"

Donny spoke into the mike again. "I'm saying that you need to meet us, and I want you to make sure that you're alone. If you're concerned about Jacob's well-being, do not contact the authorities."

"My well-being?" I said. What was he talking about?

Donny turned to me and gave me a very hard look. It was as if he were a totally different person.

"This is crazy!" my father said.

"I can understand your surprise, Doctor. But do you understand my message clearly?"

"I'm not sure."

"Jacob's life depends on your *not*, I repeat *not*, contacting the authorities. You are to show up at dawn alone. Do you copy?"

There was a hesitation, then my father's voice very quietly saying, "I copy."

"Good!" Donny said. "We'll have time to discuss the details when we meet. A bright man like you should be able to figure out what I want. But more on that tomorrow morning."

"Okay, okay . . ."

"One more thing," Donny said. "We'll be monitoring your radio, as we have been for the past several months. So don't try anything stupid. Jacob says goodbye." He hung the mike back on the instrument panel and flicked off the radio, then turned to me.

I stared at him in utter shock. I couldn't believe the conversation I'd just heard.

"I have not been very truthful with you," he said. "You gave my men a very bad time—killed one actually. But I'm not worried about that."

I glanced down at the spear between the seat.

"Don't be stupid," he said. "Unless you can fly an airplane, that would be a mistake. Just relax, enjoy the flight. If things go well tomorrow you and your father will be together again, and I will have my elephants."

Twenty-two

As we flew away from my father's camp, Supeet's words echoed through my mind: *"Evil is smart—never forget this."* How could I have been so stupid? *"My wife and I are big fans of his. . . . If I had guns on this baby, I'd blow them to hell."* And what did he mean by *"and I will have my elephants"*? I wanted to see my father, but not like this.

Donovan, or whatever his real name was, flew over the valley where the cave was. The cloud seemed to be growing. At least I could take some satisfaction in knowing that I'd helped Supeet with the rain ceremony.

"I don't think I'll go over the top of that," Donovan said, nodding at the cloud. "We better go around. We're setting up a temporary camp at the rendezvous site. We'll spend the night, and tomorrow morning, after your dad shows up, this will be all over."

"What'll be all over?" I asked.

He smiled. "You'll see soon enough."

No doubt, I thought, and looked out my side of the airplane. When we reached the end of the valley he banked left and flew over the east hill. On the other side was the escarpment road. He paralleled it for ten minutes, then reduced the power.

"This is the place," he said.

Below were a couple of trucks and a jeep. Several

193

men were setting up tents. Donovan swung the airplane around, eased the nose up, and came in for a landing. He taxied the airplane to the trucks and shut the engine off.

He turned to me. "I don't know how you managed to escape before, but it's not going to happen again. If your Masai friend shows up he will die. If you try to get away you will die. And . . . ," he grabbed my shirt and looked right in my face, "your father will die! Do you understand?"

I nodded.

"We could have killed your father anytime we wanted to," he continued. "We've been monitoring his radio calls for a long time. He knows what we want, but he's been very clever about that—very clever. That's all over now because we have you." He pushed me away from him.

"What do you want?" I asked.

He looked surprised, then laughed. "You really don't know, do you?"

I shook my head.

"Ivory," he said. "Your father has radio collared a herd of elephants with the biggest tusks in Africa. He's the only one who knows where they are, and tomorrow he's going to lead us to them."

That explained why my father had been so secretive about his location and why the institute couldn't reach him. He must have known that the poachers were monitoring the radio.

The airplane door opened, and I turned around. Standing there was Moja.

"So we meet again." He smiled, then yanked me out of the plane and threw me on the ground.

Just as he was about to kick me, Donovan said, "Not so rough, Moja!" He climbed out after me. "After all, Jacob is the one who is responsible for leading us to the prize."

Moja looked irritated, but he didn't plant his boot in my side. Instead, he barked some orders at the two men standing next to him. They pushed me over on my stomach, pulled my arms back roughly, and tied my wrists.

"Secure him outside the cook tent," Donovan said to Moja. "I want two men guarding him at all times. No one is to talk to him except you and me. If he causes a problem in the camp tonight, the first thing I want your men to do is shoot him. No questions, no hesitation—is that understood?"

Moja nodded and translated the orders for the two men. They picked me up by my arms and dragged me to the tent. A metal stake had been driven into the ground outside the entrance. They pushed me down and tied my wrists to it, then took up positions on either side of me.

I watched as the men put up tents and built a fire in the middle of the camp. From one of the trucks they unloaded a tall telescoping antenna and hammered stakes into the ground for guide wires. Another man put a table near the antenna and set up a radio. He slipped on a pair of headphones and fooled with the dial. This was no doubt how they monitored my father's calls and probably every other radio call in the area. No wonder they hadn't been caught. They knew exactly what everyone was doing and could stay one step ahead of them.

The first camp I'd been taken to must have been

nothing more than a processing plant. What I was seeing now was the command center. The men in this camp were professionals. *"Evil is smart—never forget this."*

Another table was unloaded and carried over to the tent where I was tied. A man came out of the tent, said something to the man with the table, and together they positioned it under the awning. He went back into the tent and came out a moment later with a white tablecloth, which he put over the table. On his next trip he came out with an armful of dishes and silverware and carefully set the table with two place settings.

I couldn't believe it. They had to have a tremendous amount of money to set up something like this in the middle of nowhere.

I looked at the fire. Another man had set up a grill over the fire and was unloading a huge box of pots and pans. Donovan had a personal cook and a waiter.

After a while Donovan came out of his tent wearing a fresh safari suit. Moja walked over to Donovan, and they talked for some time. When they finished, Donovan sauntered over to where I was and looked down at me.

"You must be hungry," he said.

I was, but I didn't answer. He smiled and said to one of the guards, "You can untie him now."

The guard squatted down and took the ropes off. I brought my arms in front of me and rubbed my wrists.

"That must feel better," he said. "You're free to stand."

I got stiffly to my feet and stretched.

"I thought you might want to dine with me," he said.

"No," I said. "I don't want to *dine* with you."

"But we've set a place for you. My cook has gone to a lot of trouble for our important guest."

"I'm not going to eat your food."

"Well," he said. "I can't make you eat. But I can make you sit."

"No," I said. "I'd rather be tied up." I sat back down and put my hands behind my back.

"*My,*" he said sarcastically. "Aren't we stubborn." To one of the guards he said, "Please seat the gentleman."

The guard handed his rifle to the other guard and hauled me to my feet. Donovan pulled a chair out from the table and the guard slammed me down into it.

"That's better," Donovan said. "Much more civilized. I wouldn't enjoy my meal at all if I had to look at you tied up." He walked to the other side of the table and sat down across from me.

The waiter brought two salads out from the tent and set them in front of us. He then brought out a pitcher of water and filled our glasses. Donovan began to eat his salad. I hadn't seen lettuce since I'd been in Nairobi, but I wasn't going to eat it.

"Is there something the matter with the salad?"

Yeah, it belongs to you, I thought. But I didn't say anything. He finished his salad, then motioned for the plates to be taken away. The waiter brought the main course over in a pot from the fire. It was a meat stew with potatoes, and it smelled wonderful. My mouth watered, but I didn't lift an arm.

Donovan tasted the stew and nodded his approval. "Delicious," he said. "Don't tell me you're not going to eat the stew, either."

"I told you that I'm not going to eat anything of yours."

"That's very admirable, Jacob. But also very stupid. You must at least drink some water. We can't have you dying of thirst in the middle of the night."

"No," I said. I wasn't going to die of thirst, but I wished I could. If I died they'd have nothing to hold over my father, and they might not find the elephants. "I'm not afraid of dying."

"Everyone is afraid to die," he said. "In fact the fear of dying is the one common denominator everyone shares."

That's because they haven't died before, I thought. And I realized how lucky I was to understand that there was something on the other side. I wondered if death was the same for everyone. When Donovan died would there be a warm white light and a feeling of incredible well-being? Or was that experience something that belonged just to me?

"You must drink some water," he said. "We did not poach it, and it has been purified. It's quite good."

"No thanks," I said.

"You're a very difficult boy!" He was irritated, and I was glad that I was getting to him. "Bring me his water gourd!"

One of the guards ran off and came back a moment later with Supeet's gourd. He handed it to me.

"Our water is probably better," Donovan said. "But if you prefer you can drink your own."

I smiled and thought of Supeet and thanked him silently for the water, then tilted my head back and took a long drink.

Donovan ate the rest of his meal in silence. When he was finished he stood up. "Oh, one more thing," he said, reaching into his jacket pocket. He pulled out a small stack of letters and tossed them on the table. "Your father's mail," he said. "Kenya's postal system really stinks. You can deliver them to him tomorrow." He turned to the guard and said, "When he's finished tie him back up." He started to walk away, then stopped and looked back at me. "We were very sorry to hear about your mother," he said, and continued across the camp to his tent.

I watched him walk away, then looked at the letters on the table. They'd all been opened. Four of the letters were from me, the fifth letter was from my mother. Donovan had known all along why I was in Kenya. I unfolded my mother's letter to my father. It was dated a week before she died.

Dear Robert,

Things are fine on the home front, but your son misses you terribly. The walls are covered with the photos you send. When you write to him he marks your camp on the map and dates it.

Jacob has turned into a wonderful young man. Like you, he has a serious side and an outrageous side. And he is brighter than both of us put together. You and I may not have been suited for one another, but we did manage to produce a very special human being. He will do great things one day—I'm sure of it. Please come home soon; you're missing the evolution of something wonderful.

Love,
Beth

I put my head down on the table to hide my tears.

Twenty-three

I heard the clatter of pots and pans and opened my eyes. It was still dark out, but the men were already moving around camp. The fire had been stoked, and the cook was busy making breakfast. Before long, Donovan came out of his tent.

I was very nervous about meeting my father. They'd probably been intercepting his mail for months, and there was a good chance that he didn't know about my mother's death. What was I going to say to him? How was I going to break the news about Mom?

I was also nervous about Supeet. By now he must have come out of his trance and discovered I was gone. What would this do to the ceremony? From where I was sitting the sky looked clear.

Donovan walked over. "Good morning."

I looked up at him. "My father doesn't know about my mother, does he?"

"No, I don't believe he does. He's been pretty isolated."

"The institute has tried to reach him on the radio," I said.

"But they stopped trying. We jammed all of his incoming signals."

"Why?"

"He knows where the elephants are. We've tried to follow him to the elephants, but he's managed to elude us. Your father knows what we want, but he won't give in. He has only one native working with him, and I don't think even *he* knows where those elephants are."

"Why didn't you kidnap him and make him tell you?"

Donovan laughed. "Come, Jacob. You know your father better than I do. Do you think he'd tell us?"

No I didn't. "What makes you think he'll tell you now?"

"He'll tell us to protect you. He cares more about you than he does about the elephants. We read the letters he sent to you before sending them on—that is, most of them. Some had just too much information, and we were unable to forward them."

They controlled everything. "Why these elephants?" I asked. "There are other elephants—"

"Not like these." He squatted in front of me. "The tusks on these elephants are worth more than you can imagine. We have a client who is going to pay a great deal for them, because he knows that they are the last of the biggest."

Donovan stood up and looked out at the lightening sky, then turned back to me. "This isn't your fault," he said. "Your father would have eventually made a mistake, or the elephants would have made a mistake. In fact, we have a pretty good idea where the elephants are. So you see it was only a matter of time."

Donovan didn't know where they were. That's why he needed my father. If my father knew they were trying to follow him to the elephants, why didn't he leave the area? And if they found the elephants on their own, what could he do to stop them from killing them? *"Your dad's pretty damn stubborn."* That answered both questions about my father. And I knew Donovan was right—to save me, my father would lead them to the elephants. It was working out perfectly for them.

"It'll be dawn soon," he said. "Your father left his camp a couple of hours ago. He should be here right on time." He walked away.

The waiter set the table again; this time he put out three place settings. The man monitoring the radio took the headset off and walked over to Donovan's tent. Donovan appeared in the doorway, and they spoke for a moment, then the man returned to the radio and Donovan walked over to me.

"Your father will be here in a moment," he said. "Untie him." I stood up and rubbed my arms. "Please sit at the table, Jacob."

I saw no point in resisting—one of the guards would just force the issue. I pulled out a chair and sat. Donovan sat down in the chair next to me.

Pretty soon I saw headlights appear in the distance. Two men with rifles ran to the edge of camp. My father's Land Rover slowed down and stopped. It was too dark to see clearly, but when he got out it looked like they frisked him. When they were finished they led him over to the tent.

"Dad!" I stood up.

Donovan reached out and grabbed my arm. "That's far enough."

"Get your hands off him!" my father shouted, and he started to move forward but was pulled back by the two guards.

"Everybody just settle down," Donovan said, still holding my arm.

"Are you all right, Jake?"

"I'm fine."

"Sit down, Jacob," Donovan said. I remained standing. "I said, sit down!" He tried to pull me down, but I resisted.

"Go ahead, son," my father said. "Do what he says." Reluctantly, I sat down.

"That's better," Donovan said. "Much better. There is no use in making this more difficult than it has to be."

I hadn't seen my father in over two years. His hair was very long and pulled back into a ponytail, and he had lost weight. He looked worried and very tense.

"I don't know how you got hold of Jake, but—"

Donovan interrupted him. "Dr. Lansa, I'll do the talking. Please sit down."

My father hesitated, then pulled out a chair and sat. The two men stared at each other. Neither spoke while the cook put food on our plates.

"Eat," Donovan finally said.

My father looked down at the plate, then at me. I kept my hands in my lap.

"Are we going to go through this again?" Donovan asked. "Your son doesn't seem to like my food, either."

For the first time since he arrived, my father smiled. It had been a long time since I had seen that smile, and it made me feel very good. "Go ahead and eat, Jake," he said. "It doesn't matter." He slowly picked up his knife and fork and began to slice the meat on the plate.

I still kept my hands in my lap. He hadn't told me to eat my food since I was kid. He forked a piece of meat into his mouth and chewed it slowly and swallowed. He turned to me again. "Jake, eat. It's all right."

I picked up my silverware and started to eat.

"Good," Donovan said. "I knew we'd be able to work through these problems."

My father looked at him. "What do you want?"

Donovan took a bite of food. "You know what I want, Dr. Lansa."

My father continued to eat. His expression gave nothing away.

"I want those elephants," Donovan continued. "And you know where they are. If you show us we'll give you Jacob. A simple exchange for something that you know we'll eventually get anyway."

"I don't know where they are," my father said.

"Dr. Lansa, let's not play games. Even we know they're near this area."

"Then send your men out and kill them, and Jacob and I will be on our way."

"As you know, it's not that simple. My trackers say the elephants disappear. I don't believe them of course. The elephants have to go somewhere, and I believe that you know where this is."

"I don't," my father said. "I have a radio collar on one of them, but I haven't heard the signal in over a week. From time to time they *do* disappear. I have no idea where they go."

"But you believe they go somewhere?"

"Yes, but I don't know where it is. They're not like other elephants. There's very little logic to their behavior." It looked like he was telling the truth—he really didn't know where they were.

Donovan thought about this for a few moments. "But you've been able to get close enough to put a collar on one."

"I got lucky. We ran into them in the bush, and I

got a dart into one before the herd ran away. They're very wary of people. I've only seen them a couple of times myself. They're almost unapproachable. I suppose that's why they've lived as long as they have."

"Well, I hope you're lucky again, Dr. Lansa," Donovan said staring at him. "Because your son's life depends on it."

My father met his gaze. "There's no guarantee that we'll find them."

Donovan looked at me. "That would be a shame."

My father sighed with resignation. "How do you want to do this?"

"We can use my airplane," Donovan said. "Attach your radio antenna to the wing. We'd cover a lot of territory in a very short time."

"Yeah," my father said distractedly. He knew that Donovan had him beat, and I knew it was my fault. I felt awful. My father got a distant look on his face as if he was thinking about something, then turned to Donovan and said quietly, "I realize that I'm in no position to bargain, but let me run something by you."

"Go ahead," Donovan said cautiously.

"You've killed most of the elephants around here. Certainly all the big tuskers—"

Donovan interrupted. "Not all of them—"

"Please let me finish," my father said.

"By all means." Donovan seemed amused. "But before you continue let me tell you something. Perhaps it will make you feel better. As you know, large tusks are rare and there are collectors who will pay a great deal for the tusks. The ivory from your elephants will not be cut up into small pieces—the collectors want them kept whole."

"That doesn't make me feel any better," my father said. "This herd represents a genetic line that can't be replaced. Do you know what that means?"

"No, but I'm sure that you'll tell me," Donovan said sarcastically.

"What you're doing is killing the goose that laid the golden egg," my father continued. "You've killed all the big tuskers. The only elephants left are the ones that were passed over because their ivory wasn't worth taking. If you kill all the elephants with big tusks, then there will be no more big ivory. Big ivory is inherited, passed from one generation to another."

"Are you suggesting that we let these elephants go?" Donovan asked.

"No," my father said. "I realize that you're holding all the cards, and you won't do that."

"I'm glad you see it my way."

"What I'm suggesting is that you let me tranquilize the elephants. When they're down I'll cut the tusks off. There'll be some damage and a great deal of pain for the elephants, but this way they might survive."

"Innovative, Dr. Lansa. Very innovative." Donovan looked across the savanna and tapped his fingertips together as he thought about this. After several seconds he looked back at my father and said, "And if I do this, what will I get out of it?"

"Aside from doing something decent?"

"Yes, aside from that."

It was my father's turn to think. He stood up, walked a few steps from the table, then turned around. "I'll cooperate," he said.

"But I already have your cooperation," he said. "I have your son."

"I mean I'll *really* cooperate," my father said, regaining some of his passion. "I'll try to locate the elephants as quickly as possible. I'll use every trick I know to get close to them, and you have my word that we won't try to escape. You know these elephants are nervous. I promise you that I won't try to spook them."

He came back to the table and sat down. "I haven't been exactly straight with you," he said.

"That doesn't surprise me, Dr. Lansa."

"I've been around the herd a lot," he said. "Three of them are collared, not one. I've been close enough to take individual photos of all of them."

"So it hasn't been luck?"

"No," he said. "They sometimes tolerate my being around. It's as if they know I don't mean them any harm. And there are other times . . ." My father shook his head. "Well, they're just spooky, and I can't get within miles of them. Their signal goes off the air. I have no idea where they go. Then one day I pick up the signal again."

"And you're able to get close again?"

"Sometimes, sometimes not," my father said. "But I'll tell you one thing; if you start blasting them with your rifles, you'll get one, maybe two, but you won't get the whole herd. They'll disappear into the bush, and you'll never see them again."

Donovan looked at my father and smiled. "You know, Dr. Lansa, you think on your feet. I admire that. And I think that you've given me another genetics lesson as well."

"What's that?"

Donovan pointed at me. "Your son, of course," he said. "He is very much like you. He frightened a herd of elephants away from us, and he made a very daring escape despite being guarded by two men. You are very much alike. I guess you'd say it's in the genes."

My father looked at me. "You scared elephants away from them?"

I nodded.

He grinned, then looked at Donovan. "Well?"

"We will try it your way because it amuses me," Donovan said. "But don't forget that I *do* hold all of the cards and that both you and your son will die if you betray me." Donovan stood up. "And that will end *your* genetic line."

My father looked at him. "What guarantee do I have that you'll let us go when this is over?"

Donovan said, "When we get the ivory from these elephants, our work is finished in this part of Africa. There's nothing more worth taking. As we speak, the ivory is being loaded and will be taken to a depository where it will be shipped out of the country. By the time you and Jacob can report this, it will be as if we were never here."

"Except for the bones you've left behind," I said.

Donovan looked at me and smiled pleasantly, then looked back at my father. "You see, Dr. Lansa, it is genetic."

He stood up and called Moja. Moja walked to the tent.

"Dr. Lansa is now in charge of this operation," Donovan said. "I want you to do everything he asks."

Moja acknowledged the order with a slight nod, but he didn't look too happy about it.

Twenty-four

My father swung into action, as I'd seen him do many times before at the zoo.

"The first thing we'll have to do is rig the airplane," he said. "My gear's in the Land Rover. Have one of your men bring it over."

"Fine," Moja said, and walked away.

My father, Donovan, and I walked to the airplane with the two guards close behind. Moja drove up in the Land Rover, and my father unloaded the gear.

"How does all this work?" Donovan asked.

"Pretty simple," my father said as he began to screw together an antenna. "The three elephants are wearing collars with transmitters attached to them. Each transmitter sends out a signal on a different frequency. We punch in their number on the receiver, and when we hear their signal, we can get a location on them. Here, I'll show you."

He attached the small antenna to a handheld receiver, then he reached into the Land Rover and pulled out a black metal box the size of a shoe box and handed it to Donovan. "That's the transmitter," he said.

Donovan tested its weight. "It's heavy."

"So are elephants. The smaller the animal the smaller the transmitter. Most of the size and weight is from the battery that runs the transmitter. The transmitters are attached to heavy canvas collars. The reason we use canvas is that eventually the canvas rots and the collar comes off so the elephant doesn't have to wear it forever."

"How long do the batteries last?"

"Couple of years," my father said. "Sometimes more, sometimes less. Depends. Do you see the number on the transmitter?"

Donovan nodded.

"That's the frequency number. There's a magnet on the side of the transmitter. Take it off."

Donovan removed the small gray magnet.

"Removing the magnet activates the transmitter."

My father flipped a switch on the receiver and pointed the antenna at the black box. He turned the receiver dials, and we heard a steady *beep . . . beep . . . beep* over the small built-in speaker. He switched it off.

"In the airplane we'll use headphones because of the noise. On the ground it's generally quiet enough to hear the signal over the speaker."

"What's the range of the signal?" Donovan asked.

"Depends on the contour of the land, the weather, where the elephants are—a lot of different things. The range is much greater from the air than it is from the land because you're above the hills and the signal isn't interrupted."

My father unhooked the antenna from the receiver and took it over to the airplane. "I'll attach the antenna to the wing strut and run a cable inside." He took black electrical tape and attached the antenna securely, then hooked up the receiver. "Let's test this thing and make sure it works. Jake, take the transmitter and go out a little ways."

Donovan handed me the transmitter, and I jogged out about twenty yards from the airplane. My father turned on the receiver, and we heard the signal.

"Okay," he said, switching the receiver off. I ran back. "Put the transmitter back in the Land Rover. If we dart an uncollared elephant we'll put a collar on it. I've got a couple of spares."

Always the biologist, I thought. He wouldn't pass up an opportunity to further his research no matter what the circumstances were.

"What now, Dr. Lansa?" Donovan asked.

My father thought for a moment, then said, "Okay, this is how we'll do it. We'll find the elephants, land nearby if we can, and radio in our location. Your men will meet us at the airplane with my Land Rover and a truck for the ivory, and I'll get my tranquilizer gear together. Do you have water?"

"Yes."

"We'll need it to cool the elephant down while it's tranquilized. They tend to overheat, and I don't want to lose one. Have your men bring several large containers filled with water."

Donovan looked at Moja, who nodded like he understood.

"Shall we go then?"

"One more thing," my father said. "The fewer people the better. One man in the truck, one man in the Land Rover. We don't need any more than this."

"That will be fine, Dr. Lansa," Donovan said. "Young Jacob will remain here."

"No way!" my father said. "He's not leaving my sight, or the deal's off!"

Donovan thought about this for a moment. "In

that case," he said, "we'll take Moja with us to keep Jacob company. And I must tell you that Moja is not very fond of Jacob and would like nothing more than to end his life."

My father ignored his remark. "Let's go and get this over with."

Moja gave the two guards some orders, then we all climbed into the airplane. I crawled in back and Moja got in next to me. Donovan got into the pilot's seat, and my father got in next to him.

Donovan started the airplane. From the back I watched as my father attached the cable to the receiver and slipped on a headset so he could hear the signal above the noise of the engine. I wondered when we'd have time to talk. And what would I say to him about my mother? I had so many things to tell him. Donovan taxied out into the open and took off.

In a few minutes we were in the air. It was light out, and for the first time since I'd arrived, the sky was overcast.

I couldn't hear what my father and Donovan were saying above the engine noise. Every once in a while my father gave a hand signal and Donovan eased the airplane in the direction he was pointing. We made several very wide circles, then my father pointed straight ahead. We flew over the top of the east hill where the cave was located, and my father directed him to fly in another circle. My father nodded and said something, and Donovan cut the engines and started to bring the airplane down. While he was still above the hills he radioed in our position.

Donovan had been right—the elephants were

near. We hadn't been in the airplane more than fifteen minutes. He was landing in the narrow valley between the two hills. The wheels touched down, and we rolled over the savanna.

"I guess your luck is good, Dr. Lansa," he said, after he turned the engine off.

"We'll see," my father said grimly. "Finding them was easy." He opened the door and jumped out. The rest of us followed.

My father took the antenna off the wing and attached it to the receiver and pointed it east above his head. *Beep . . . beep . . . beep . . .*

"They're in the hills," he said. "They don't seem to be moving much. That's good. I might be able to get close, but we'll have to wait for my gear."

Donovan looked at his watch. "It should be here within an hour."

My father turned the receiver off and looked at me. "Okay," he said. "Why are you here?"

I didn't answer. I wasn't sure that this was the right time to get into it. My father saw my hesitation and turned to Donovan. "How about some privacy," he said.

Donovan didn't move and didn't respond.

"I gave you my word that I'd cooperate," my father said angrily.

"I suppose there's nothing you can do," he said. "You may take a short walk. No more than twenty-five feet away." He turned to Moja. "If they go farther, or try to run, shoot the boy in the back."

Moja smiled and slipped his rifle's safety off.

"You won't need it," my father said. "Come on, Jake."

We walked a few yards away and stopped. "Okay, Jake. What's going on?"

I took a deep breath. "Well," I began. "First of all I'm sorry about the elephants. I've screwed everything up—"

"Don't worry about the elephants," my father said. "The poachers have been watching me for a long time, and I was just about ready to give up. They're organized and have all the resources in the world. They even had a good idea of where the elephants were." He looked toward the east hills. "If you hadn't shown up I probably wouldn't have thought of this, and they would have killed the elephants."

I wasn't convinced. "They've been taking your mail," I said.

"Yes, I thought so. I haven't gotten a letter from you or your mother in months. I figured that something was going on. They cut me off."

I nodded.

"So why are you here, Jake? Beth must be going—"

"Mom died," I said. I didn't know any other way to put it.

He looked confused. "What?"

I told him about the accident and the funeral. He listened in silence. When I finished, his shoulders began to shake and he dropped to his knees. I put my arms around him. We held each other and cried for a long time.

After a while, he pulled away and we both wiped the tears from our faces. "I loved her like I've never loved anyone," he said.

I nodded. My father stood up and glanced at the airplane, trying to regain his composure. He looked back at me. "You still haven't said why you're here. What about Sam?"

I told him the whole story. The white light, floating above Africa, meeting Supeet, Sitonik, the poachers, the rain ceremony, Lumeya's grave, the cave.

"You mean your friend Supeet's in the cave now?"

"As far as I know," I said. "The cave is in the hills to the east."

He looked at the sky, then looked back at me and grinned. "Supeet might be right," he said. "You may be here for more reasons than you know. Perhaps we all are. I'm looking forward to meeting him."

"You're going to like each other," I said.

We heard engines in the distance and looked down the valley. The Land Rover and truck were approaching rapidly.

"Well, let's get this over with," he said.

He put his arm around my shoulder, and we walked back to the airplane.

Twenty-five

My father took a tarp from the Land Rover, and I helped him spread it out on the ground. He then took out two large tackle boxes and a rifle case and set them on the tarp.

"I'll load the tranquilizer darts here," he said, opening one of the boxes. Inside were drug vials and disassembled tranquilizer darts. He pulled on a pair of surgical gloves. "Put a pair on, Jake," he said. "You know the routine."

"Why the gloves?" Donovan asked.

"We're going to use a drug called M-99," he said. "It's very dangerous. A drop in an open cut can kill you. You've got to be very careful." He picked up a vial and very carefully pulled the M-99 out with a syringe.

I took one of the dart shafts, put a charge in the feathered cap, and screwed it onto the end of the shaft. My father talked as he worked.

"We'll only be able to do one elephant at a time. But I'll load a couple of darts in case I miss. The dart rifle operates on CO_2. When the dart hits the elephant the impact ignites the charge, which pushes the plunger forward, and the drug goes in. The rifle is almost silent—just a slight popping noise. If we're lucky the elephants won't panic. They'll just wander farther into the bush. When we're done with the first elephant, we'll find the herd and do it again."

"How long is the elephant down?" Donovan asked.

"As long as we want it down. That's the beauty of M-99. There's an antidote called M-50/50. When we're finished I inject the antidote into a vein in the elephant's ear, and it'll be on its feet within minutes. The whole procedure won't take long. I have obstetrics wire that will cut through the tusks cleanly."

"Sounds pretty harmless," Donovan said.

"Not necessarily," my father said. "The elephant could have a bad reaction to the drug. And when we take the tusks off there's going to be a big hole in the tusk stump. Tusks are hollow at the base. Filled with pulp, just like your teeth. An open wound like that is an invitation to infection—and there's going to be a lot of pain." My father looked up at Donovan angrily. "So don't think that this is humane. It isn't! It's just better than your alternative."

He looked back to what he was doing and carefully filled the dart shaft I was holding with M-99. When he was finished I screwed a barbed needle onto the shaft and set the dart on the tarp. We repeated the procedure for the second dart.

My father took the two darts and put a protective sleeve over the needles so the M-99 wouldn't leak out. He opened the gun case and took the rifle out. He unscrewed the end of the CO_2 chamber and shook out the cartridge and put a new one in. He tested it by firing the rifle without a dart in it. It made a slight *pop* every time he pulled the trigger. Satisfied, he took one of the darts, slid it into the breech, and put the other dart in his pocket.

He stood up. "That's about it," he said, handing

me the rifle. He turned on the receiver and held the antenna above his head toward the east hill. *Beep ... beep ... beep ...* "They haven't moved very far." He reached for the rifle. I handed it to him, and he slung it over his shoulder. Then he slipped the receiver strap over his head so that it hung at his side.

"Well," he said, looking at the hills. "I guess I'm ready."

"What do we do?" Donovan asked.

"You wait here," he said.

"With Jacob," Donovan reminded him.

"Yeah, with Jacob," he said. "This is a job that I have to do alone."

"That's fine, Dr. Lansa," Donovan said. "We have every confidence in you, and we have your son."

"Nothing better happen to him."

Donovan smiled. "Don't worry. We are all going to get what we want today."

"It's going to take me a while to do this. So don't worry—I'll be back. If I dart one I'll come to the base of the hill and wave, then you can drive the trucks up."

"That will be fine," Donovan said.

My father looked at me and smiled. "You can put the gear away if you want."

I nodded and smiled. Putting the gear away had been my job when I was a little kid. "Good luck," I said.

"Right," he said, and walked toward the west hill across the savanna.

I watched until he disappeared into the bush at the base of the hill.

An hour and a half passed. Nobody spoke. The clouds grew thicker and darker. I tapped out the drumbeat with my foot. It was hot and humid, but at least the sun wasn't beating down on us. I wondered what my father and I would do after this was over. Would he send me back to New York, or would he let me stay? I couldn't imagine him coming to New York with me. Africa seemed to be where he belonged, and I felt that it was where I belonged as well.

I saw a movement at the base of the hill. My father came out of the bush, but he didn't wave. Instead, he walked briskly in our direction. Something had gone wrong.

The two men jumped off the tailgate and started for the doors of the truck.

"Wait," Donovan said. They stopped. "What's going on, Jacob?"

I stood up and watched my father. "I don't know," I said. "Something isn't right."

We waited for my father. He walked silently to the Land Rover, drenched in sweat. When he got there he put the rifle in the back and got the canteen and took a long drink. He looked at Donovan.

"I got up to them," he said disgustedly. "But they ran, and I couldn't get a shot off. They're very nervous today."

Donovan didn't respond.

My father continued. "It might be best to let them settle down for a while. They didn't run very far."

Donovan got out of the Land Rover and walked over to my father. He looked at the sky. "Well," he said. "It was a noble effort, Dr. Lansa."

"What do you mean?" my father asked.

"I mean that we are running out of time. It looks like rain. And that will turn this valley into a mud wallow that will make it very difficult to transport the ivory."

"We have a deal!"

"Which has just been called off on account of rain."

"No," my father said. "If you send your men after the elephants you'll only get one or two. Give me another chance."

Donovan looked at him. "You look very tired, Dr. Lansa. I imagine that you didn't get much sleep last night. You need a rest, and unfortunately, we have no time for that."

"Let me do it," I said.

All three men looked at me in surprise.

"I can do it!" I said.

"I don't think . . ." Donovan began.

"Let him finish!" my father interrupted.

I told them about stalking the rhinos and about Supeet coming into the poachers' camp.

"I wondered how you had gotten out of the camp," Donovan said. "So where is your friend now?"

"Long gone," I said. Which was true in a way.

"Let him do it," my father said. "He knows how to use the dart rifle. What do you have to lose?"

"Time, Dr. Lansa. Time." Donovan looked at his watch, then glanced at the sky. "You have one hour," he said. "If you're not back we will move in with the truck and see how many we can get."

"Okay," I said, hoping that an hour would be enough time.

My father took the rifle out of the back of the Land Rover and handed it and the spare dart to me. He reached for the antenna and receiver.

"I won't need that," I said.

"What?" He looked surprised.

"Just another thing to carry," I said. "Point out

220

where you last saw them."

He pointed. "See that narrow gully to the north?"

I nodded.

"They ran up it a little ways."

"Okay," I said, and started off.

"One hour," I heard Donovan say behind me.

"Good luck, son."

I didn't turn around to look.

To save time I jogged to the base of the hill. When I got there I looked around and found the plant Supeet had used for camouflage. I took off my clothes and rubbed the juice from the plant all over, then I rolled on the ground covering myself with dust. When I was finished I moved cautiously toward the gully and reached it in less than fifteen minutes.

I started up the gully very slowly, concentrating on everything around me. The brush became thinner the higher I went. Up ahead the path took a sharp turn to the right. Still no sign of the elephants. I began to think that I was in the wrong place, then I heard a branch snap ahead of me. I froze. Another branch snapped. Then another. The elephants were coming toward me! I took several slow steps backward and moved to my left.

I saw a glint of white through the bushes, then the top of a gray head. The elephants were within fifty feet of me, calmly moving down the gully. I tried to concentrate on what they were seeing, not what I was seeing. My arms seemed to position themselves as if they had a mind of their own—as if they knew exactly where to go. I was barely breathing. I saw myself standing like a statue against the bushes. It was just like when I had floated above myself in the dry riverbed, only the angle was different now. I was lumbering down the gully. I was seeing everything the elephants were seeing. And then I was gone! I wasn't there anymore. When the first elephant passed by I saw things from the viewpoint of the second elephant.

The elephants walked by very slowly, and when the final elephant passed by my own viewpoint returned. The rump of the last elephant was twenty feet away. I raised the rifle to my cheek and fired.

Pop! The elephant trumpeted and swung around trying to reach the dart with its trunk. I didn't move— the rifle was still at my cheek. The herd panicked and ran down the gully while the darted elephant continued to move in circles trying to get the dart out. I heard branches breaking to the north as the elephants ran. The darted elephant gave up on trying to remove the dart and headed down the gully to find the others. I followed the elephant at a safe distance. When it got to the bottom of the gully it began to stumble. It fell to its front knees, then got up again and stood still with the tip of its long trunk touching the ground. The ends of its huge tusks came within inches of the ground. The elephant raised its front foot to take a step forward but lost its balance and came crashing to the ground. It tried to get up, fell over on its side, then lay still.

I walked over and watched its chest heave with each breath. The elephant looked like it was going to be all right. I put the rifle down and ran back through the brush.

When I reached the savanna, the truck and Land Rover were already moving along the base of the hill.

I couldn't believe that an hour had passed. My father drove up in the Land Rover and stopped. Donovan and Moja were with him.

"Did you see them?" my father asked.

"I got one down," I said.

"Where?" My father was excited.

"At the end of the gully."

"Well I'll be damned!" He reached down and held up my clothes. "We found these where you went into the bush. Is that the trick?"

I took the clothes from him and grinned. "Not exactly," I said, pulling on my pants and shirt.

"Enough congratulations," Donovan said impatiently. "We have business to take care of." The truck pulled up behind us, and the other two men got out.

I put my shoes on, and my father handed me one of the tackle boxes. I led them to the elephant.

"Jacob and I will take the tusks off," my father said. "Have one of your men pour water over the elephant's ear slowly. It will help to keep it cool."

Moja said something to one of the men, and the man climbed onto the elephant's head with a water container.

"I want to do this quick," my father said. "So we can give it the antidote."

"What about putting a collar on it?" I asked.

"That will take too much time," Donovan said.

My father started to protest but then thought better of it. "Okay," he said. "Let's just get this over with. Hand me the obstetrics wire."

I got the wire out of the tackle box. He ran it underneath the lower tusk, attached a handle on each end of the wire, and began cutting.

"I smell something burning," I said.

"That's just the friction from the wire," he said. "It creates heat." He looked up at Donovan. "When I'm through the tusk, have your men pull it away. I'll have Jacob plug the cavity with gauze while I start on the other tusk."

I got the gauze out of the tackle box. "Should I put anything on this?" I asked.

"Yeah," my father said. He was sweating with exertion. "Put some Betadine on it. It won't do much good, but it will make *me* feel better. I'll give him an antibiotic shot before we give him the antidote."

I squirted Betadine onto the gauze. A moment later he was through the first tusk.

"Take it away," he said, and started cutting the other tusk.

It took the two men and Moja to pull the heavy tusk away. They put it on their shoulders and walked toward the truck. As I filled the cavity with gauze I felt something cold hit my neck. It happened again and I looked up. It was beginning to rain.

"The long rains," my father said. "This is unbelievable!"

I looked over at Donovan. He was watching the rain make small craters in the dust. He didn't look very happy, and I wished that I could tell Supeet to turn it off. Just for a few minutes, Supeet, I thought. Just until we get this job done. It began to rain harder.

Before my father finished cutting through the second tusk, he told the men to hold the end of it. "I don't want it to break off and fracture up into the socket."

They held on while he cut, and the tusk dropped

off cleanly. They took the tusk away, and I stuffed the second cavity with gauze.

"Okay," my father said. "I'm going to give it an antibiotic shot and then I'm going to give it the antidote. Get all of this gear out of here and stand back."

While he gave the antibiotic shot I packed the gear up and carried it a short distance away. Donovan, Moja, and I watched as my father stood near the elephant's head. He found a vein in the ear and slowly injected the M-50/50.

He stood back and watched the elephant for a moment, then reached down and picked up the rifle and joined us.

"This will only take a couple of minutes," he said. "Do you have that other dart?"

I handed him the dart and he reloaded the rifle. "Are you ready to do this again?" he asked.

"Sure," I said.

The elephant began to move. It swung its legs and rocked itself onto its sternum and shook its head. A moment later it got into a sitting position and slowly got to its feet. It took a step forward and almost fell, but regained its balance.

I looked at the bloody stumps. The elephant looked deformed without its magnificent tusks.

"Quite a sight, isn't it?" my father said grimly.

I looked at Donovan and Moja. They were both silent and looked angry and frustrated, but not because of the elephant. The rain was pouring down now.

Called off on account of rain? I had a feeling they weren't going to be satisfied with one elephant.

Twenty-six

We walked single file through the brush toward the truck: Donovan in the lead, followed by my father, me, then Moja. The ground was slippery, and with all the gear, walking was difficult. My father wanted to fix one more location with the receiver before we tried for another elephant. He thought that they had probably gone a long ways, but he was wrong.

As soon as we reached the savanna we saw the elephants moving east toward the opposite hills. They moved briskly, out in the open, no more than two hundred yards away.

"Shoot them!" Donovan yelled.

The two poachers in the truck looked at him like they didn't understand what he meant. Moja shouted something from behind me, and the men immediately jumped out of the truck and began scrambling for their rifles.

"No!" my father yelled and ran forward. "No!"

One of the men pointed his rifle at the elephants. My father stopped, raised the dart rifle, and fired. *Pop!* The man screamed and fell over with the dart sticking out of his neck. I heard a shot roar out from behind me, and my father crumpled to the ground. I ran over to him.

"The elephants, Jake," he said through clenched teeth. "The elephants. Where are they?"

I looked up and saw them running full speed across the valley. They'd almost reached the base of the east hills and were out of range.

"They're safe," I said.

"Good."

He'd been hit in the leg. Blood seeped out of the wound to the ground and thinned as it was met by the falling rain. I put my hand over the wound, trying to slow the bleeding.

Donovan came over and stood above us.

"That was stupid, Dr. Lansa," he said. "Very, very stupid."

I looked over at the man my father had shot. Moja and the other man were trying to help him, but it was too late. He convulsed, then lay still. Moja and the other poacher looked coldly in our direction. We were in big trouble. *"Your father's pretty damn stubborn."* No kidding.

"We had a deal," my father said.

Donovan sneered. "Not anymore."

"Those elephants are special," my father pleaded. "Don't you understand?"

"I understand all too well," Donovan said. "That's why we've gone to so much trouble."

"Sitonik said that only special animals come here."

I knew where the elephants were going! That's why my father couldn't pick up the signal at times. The elephants were going back into the cave. If the poachers tracked them there they'd be able to kill every one of them.

Moja walked over to us. "Mahega is dead," he said, and pointed his rifle down at my father.

"Don't kill him," Donovan said calmly.

Moja looked at him angrily. "Why?"

"Because someone will pay for his return."

Moja's jaw tensed, and it was obvious that he didn't like the answer. He continued to point his rifle at my father. I didn't breathe.

"He's no good to us dead," Donovan continued. "I will give you half the money that I get for him."

Moja glanced away from my father to Donovan.

"It should be a substantial amount," Donovan continued calmly. "Along with the money you're going to get for the ivory, you'll be a rich man."

Moja raised his rifle barrel. I took a breath.

"Get the truck ready," Donovan said. "We'll go after the elephants."

Moja nodded and walked away.

Donovan looked at my father. "No need to thank me, Dr. Lansa."

"You won't get away with this."

Donovan laughed. "I already have." He looked at me. "You're coming with us," he said. "We may need your help with the elephants."

"I've got to help my father," I said.

"Your father can take care of himself. He has his medical kit. Now come with me!" He pulled me away from my father, and I jerked out of his grasp. Moja came running over and pointed his rifle at me. "Take him to the truck," ordered Donovan.

"Go ahead, Jake," my father said. "I'll be fine. Do what they say."

Moja pushed me in the back with his rifle barrel. "Move!" I started walking to the truck.

I climbed into the back of the truck with the other

poacher. As we pulled away I looked back at my father. He had already opened the medical box and was dressing his wound.

The wheels of the truck slipped and spun in the mud as we drove toward the east hill where the elephants had gone. When we got to the base of the hill we had to get out and walk. The elephants' platter-size footprints led us toward the cave. We cut through the grove of yellow-fever trees and came to the baobab. They stopped at the pile of rocks around the tree. The poacher said something to Moja, and Moja shrugged.

"Lumeya's grave," I said.

Moja's expression changed—he seemed frightened. "How do you know this?"

"I know," I said.

He and the other man began talking rapidly to each other. Donovan turned around. "What's going on?" The two men ignored him, and he walked back to them. "I said, what's going on?"

"Lumeya." Moja said, pointing at the rocks.

"Who the hell's that!"

"This is not a good place," Moja said.

"What do you mean?" Donovan was angry. "This is where the elephants are. Let's go!"

The three men began to shout at each other. I stepped away from them. They didn't seem to notice. I took another step. They continued to argue. Another step. They didn't pay attention. I started to run toward the cave. Behind me the shouting came to an abrupt end, and I knew they had discovered I had slipped away.

I got to the path leading to the cave and started

up. I didn't know what I was going to do once I got there, but I had to do something.

Outside the entrance I paused. The elephants were inside. I could see their silhouettes moving around. Since the ceremony had worked, it occurred to me that Supeet might not even be there anymore. I looked over the edge and saw the three men running toward the path. Too late to go back; I had to go inside. I kicked my tennis shoes off and moved very slowly through the entrance. The entire herd milled around inside. The sound of their rumblings echoed off the cave walls like thunder. I put my back to the wall and moved counterclockwise around the cave. There wasn't time to move slowly. The poachers would be at the entrance any second. Twice elephants brushed against me. I froze and held my breath, thinking that I was going to be crushed to death, but both times the elephants moved away. After what seemed like an eternity I reached the tunnel leading to the cavern. I crawled through it.

Rain poured in from the hole in the ceiling. Supeet was in the same position that I had left him, sitting cross-legged next to the fire, which was nothing more than wet ashes now. He had his head thrown back, letting the rain pour over his face.

"Supeet!"

He didn't move.

"Supeet!" I went over to him and shook his shoulder. "Supeet!" He brought his head forward and opened his eyes. The swelling was completely gone. "You can see!"

"Nkokua," he said, holding his hands under the water. "The long rains."

"I know," I said. "I know, but we've got problems. There are elephants in the cave."

"Yes," he said. "They arrived some time ago."

"You don't understand," I said. "The poachers are on their way up the path. They could be at the entrance by now."

He still didn't seem concerned. "It's not a good place for them to be."

"It's not a good place for us to be!" I shouted. "It's a dead end. They're going to kill the elephants and then they're going to kill us."

"It is not a dead end," he said calmly.

"There's another way out of here?"

"No," he said. "Only the way you came in. Go look."

I didn't know what he was talking about, but I ran over to the tunnel and looked anyway. I saw the elephants ambling around, then I saw two poachers arrive. They were backlit in the entrance and looked like shadows.

I turned to Supeet. "They're here," I whispered.

"Good," he said. "Are they at the entrance?"

"Yes."

"Borrow," he said.

"What do you mean? They're going to shoot the elephants."

"I think not," he said. "Borrow."

I had no idea what he was talking about, but then I understood. Borrow! Of course! I took a deep breath, and I let out the loudest bloodcurdling scream that I could. My scream was joined by the elephants' trumpeting. The ground shook. I looked down the tunnel and watched as the elephants stampeded out through the entrance like a barrage of cannonballs.

And then it was quiet. The only thing I could hear was the water trickling inside the cavern. I turned. Supeet got to his feet and walked over to me.

"I think this is yours," he said. He handed me the kachina doll.

I turned the doll over in my hand. "But I gave it to . . ."

"Sitonik wants you to thank your grandfather for loaning it to us."

"But Sitonik's dead," I said quietly.

"Yes," Supeet said. "He is with the other kachinas."

"My father!" I said. "We've got to get to him."

"Yes."

Supeet crawled through the tunnel first. I waited until he was through, then crawled through myself. By the time I got into the cave, Supeet was standing outside of the entrance. I joined him. He pointed down. Moja and the other poacher were lying on the rubble at the bottom of the cliff. I looked for Donovan but didn't see him.

"Donovan must have gotten away," I said.

Supeet began running down the path. I followed him. We passed the baobab and ran through the grove. When we got to the other side of the grove I heard the sound of the truck wheels spinning. I looked to my right and saw that Donovan had gotten the truck stuck in the soft mud of the savanna.

Supeet pointed at the Land Rover near the airplane. "Is that your father's vehicle?"

"Yeah," I said. "But I don't know how to drive. I'm a New Yorker."

Supeet laughed. "I can drive," he said "I'm

Masai." We started running across the savanna.

As we ran I looked back at Donovan and the truck. He was still stuck but seemed to be making progress. When we got to the airplane I looked again. He was moving slowly toward us across the savanna. Supeet got into the Land Rover and I started to climb in next to him, then stopped.

I went to the airplane and got Supeet's spear. I put it in the Land Rover and checked Donovan's progress. There's time, I thought. I wanted to leave a little sur- prise for Donny. I pulled something out of the Land Rover and jogged back to the airplane.

"Hurry, Jacob," Supeet said. "We must go."

"This will only take a second," I said, finishing up. I jumped in the Land Rover, and we drove off.

Halfway to my father, I looked back and saw that Donovan had reached the airplane. He was already inside and had switched on the engine.

Supeet drove to where my father was, and we got out of the Land Rover.

"How are you?" I asked, looking at the bandage around his leg.

"Okay," he said. "What's going on?"

"Moja and the other one are dead," I said.

"And Donovan's going to get away," he said dis- gustedly. We watched as Donovan brought the air- plane around facing south. It began to move forward and gathered speed. The nose left the ground, and he took off.

"He's probably going to fly to the place where he has the ivory stored," my father said. "Wherever that is."

I reached into the Land Rover and took out the

tracking receiver and antenna. I handed them to my father.

"What's this for?"

"Try frequency one-two-seven," I said. "Point the antenna south."

"But the elephants are to the east."

"I know," I said. "But the airplane is to the south."

He turned the receiver on and held the antenna above his head. The signal from the transmitter I had attached to the airplane came in loud and clear, *beep . . . beep . . . beep. . . .*

"Donny's going to be surprised," I said.

"He sure as hell will be," my father said. "Get me into the Land Rover. We've got to get back to camp!"

Twenty-seven

The wheels of the Land Rover slipped and spun over the muddy savanna. Twice we got stuck, and I had to get out and push. My father sat in back with his injured leg stretched out, trying to keep it stabilized, but every time we hit a bump he winced in pain and by the time we got to camp he was in pretty bad shape. I expected to see my father's assistant, Ngunzu, when we drove up, but the camp looked abandoned.

"Where's Ngunzu?" I asked.

"Gone," my father said. "Before I left I told him to wait until I was at Donovan's camp, then go and get help. It's going to be a while though, because he was on foot."

Supeet and I helped him out of the back of the Land Rover.

"We've got to get in touch with the Anti-Poaching Unit," my father said.

"But the radio signals are jammed," I said.

"I don't think so. My guess is that Donovan is on the move. He knows we're going to be after him, and he'll want to get the ivory out of the country as fast as he can."

We helped him over to the radio, and he began trying to reach the authorities. After twenty minutes a man came on the radio. The signal was weak, and we could barely hear him over the static, but he said that he could hear us just fine.

My father explained what had happened.

"Where do you think the ivory is? Over," the man on the radio asked.

"I don't know where it is," my father said impatiently. "Donovan was heading south. I suspect that he has the ivory cached near the Tanzanian border. We have a transmitter on his airplane. If you send a plane we can start flying around and maybe we'll get lucky. Over."

"We will send an airplane," the man said. "Is there anything else? Over."

"No. Just hurry, or—"

"Wait a second," I interrupted. My father looked at me questioningly. I held out my hand for the microphone, and he gave it to me. "My father's hurt," I said. "He's been shot in the leg, and he needs medical assistance. Over."

"I'll be fine, Jake."

I ignored him. "Did you copy that?"

"Yes," the man said. "Your father has been shot and needs medical assistance. We will send an air ambulance. Anything else? Over."

I looked at my father, and he shook his head.

"No," I said. "Over and out."

There was nothing we could do until help arrived. I convinced my father to lie down and rest in his tent. Then Supeet and I ate, and Supeet fell asleep.

I should have been tired, but I wasn't. I borrowed some of my father's clothes and walked to a small stream about a mile from camp. "The bathing hole," my father called it. The stream was already swollen with water from the long rains, which were still pouring down. I stripped and took a bath, washing away several days of sweat and dirt, and put my father's clothes on. They were too big for me, but at least they were clean. Just as I was slipping on my tennis shoes, a small airplane passed low overhead and came in for a landing near the camp. I started to jog back. Halfway there I saw a man get out of the plane and walk to my father's tent.

When I stepped into the tent the man stopped talking and looked at me. He was tall, lean, and muscular like a Masai, but instead of traditional clothing he wore a crisp khaki uniform and carried a holstered pistol on his hip. My father lay on the cot with his head propped up on his elbow. "Gilisho," he said, "this is my son, Jake."

Gilisho smiled, then turned back to my father. "The reason I'm alone is that when the call came in I was the only one there. As you know, priorities have changed. Most of our units are to the north. The drought is very bad there, and the people are killing many animals for food." He glanced outside the tent. "This rain should help."

"Well," my father said. "Under the circumstances you can't blame them for poaching. This Donovan character is another story though."

I wondered where Supeet was. I hadn't seen him when I came into camp.

"Why didn't you tell us about this problem earlier?" Gilisho asked.

"I couldn't get through," my father said. "They jammed the radio, and I was afraid to leave because I thought they'd move in on the elephants. I was even afraid to send Ngunzu out of fear they'd kill him. We rarely saw them, but we knew they were watching us. The only thing we could do was to try to lead them away from the elephants."

Gilisho nodded and said, "Tell me about this man."

My father told him everything he knew about Donovan's poaching operation.

When he was finished, Gilisho said that he thought he knew who Donovan was. "He may have been here several years ago, during the last drought. It was very profitable for him. We didn't know about it until after he had left the country."

"Well, he came back for seconds," my father said disgustedly. "And I don't think you'll be able to take him on your own."

"I won't be alone," Gilisho said, and took a map out of his back pocket and spread it out on the floor below my father's cot. Three places along the Tanzanian border were marked in red.

"We have military patrols in each of these locations. It seems likely that he is near one of these sites because there are good roads for transporting the ivory out of the country. But we don't know which one and the areas are large."

My father looked at the map for a few moments, then pointed and said, "I'd start at Lake Natron. Donovan didn't have much fuel when he took off. I don't think he could have reached the other places."

"And the transmitter?" Gilisho asked.

"You should be able to pick up the signal from at least ten miles away."

"You won't be able to come with me?" Gilisho asked.

My father pointed to his leg. "I'm afraid not."

"I can't track and fly at the same time," Gilisho said. "I'll have to wait for someone to help—"

"There's no time for that," my father interrupted. "Jake knows how to use the equipment. He'll go with you."

Gilisho glanced at me, then looked back at my father and said, "But he's just a boy."

"He put the damn transmitter on Donovan's airplane!" my father said angrily. "You don't have any choice."

"But a boy . . . ," Gilisho started to protest, when Supeet stepped into the tent.

A voice behind us said, "There are no boys here." We all turned.

"And who are you?" Gilisho asked.

Supeet didn't answer. Gilisho noticed the necklace and the snake amulet around his neck. He stared at them for a long time.

"Jacob is no longer a boy," Supeet said.

"Are those the Enkidong?" he asked.

Supeet nodded.

Gilisho glanced at me, then looked back at Supeet and said quietly, "All right."

"That settles it then," my father said.

"But what about you?" I asked him. I wanted to make sure that he got to a hospital.

"I'll be fine," he said. "I'm sure the air ambulance will be here soon."

"I'll stay with your father," Supeet added.

I looked at Gilisho and said, "I guess we can go then."

* * *

I mounted the antenna under the left wing of the airplane, then climbed into the cockpit next to Gilisho. When we were airborne I turned the receiver on and slipped the headphones over my ears and began listening for the signal.

It took us forty-five minutes to reach the Lake Natron area. I motioned for Gilisho to start circling and closed my eyes so I could listen for the signal without being distracted by what I saw outside. But I didn't hear it. We flew a few miles away and started circling again—still no signal. It was going to be dark in a couple of hours, and I was getting worried. If we didn't find Donovan before sunset, we'd have to wait until the next morning, and by then he could have the ivory out of the country.

"Perhaps they're not here," Gilisho said.

Or maybe Donovan discovered the receiver and smashed it, I thought. "Let's move a few miles east," I said.

Gilisho banked the airplane and headed east. I waited ten minutes, then tapped him on the shoulder and motioned for him to start circling again. About halfway through the loop I heard what I thought was a very faint *beep*. I had Gilisho repeat the maneuver and I heard the *beep* again.

"I think I've got a signal," I said.

Gilisho smiled. "Where?"

"Go around again." I wanted to be certain of the direction. This time I looked out the window while I listened. When I heard the *beep* I picked a landmark in the distance.

I pointed through the windshield. "Head toward that hill."

The hill was about twenty miles away. The closer we got to it the stronger the signal. "I think we've got him," I said. "He has to be near that hill."

"Good," Gilisho said, then turned the airplane sharply in the opposite direction.

"What are you doing?" I protested. "I said they're somewhere near that hill."

"We need to get help."

"Can't you use your radio?"

"And warn them that we're coming?"

He was right of course. Donovan would no doubt be monitoring all the radio traffic in the area.

"One of the military patrols is close by," he continued. "We'll land and talk to them, then we'll all go in together."

Twenty minutes later we spotted the military patrol. Gilisho flew directly over the bivouac, waggling his wings, then came in for a landing on a nearby road.

"What's the military doing out here?" I asked.

"Patrolling the border," Gilisho answered. "There are a lot of refugees coming in from Tanzania. The military is supposed to stop them, but there are too many of them. We think Donovan used the confusion to smuggle the ivory out of the country the last time he was here. But this time, because of you, we may capture him."

"At least his airplane," I said.

Gilisho laughed. "Oh, I don't think he'll be too far from his airplane."

A man picked us up in a Land Rover and drove us

over to the camp. There were at least fifty men milling around, talking and laughing. Some of them wore rain ponchos over their camouflage fatigues and flak vests. Several transport trucks were parked at the edge of camp, as well as three large helicopters.

Gilisho asked to see the captain, and we were told that he would be available soon. While we were waiting they offered us some food.

Pretty soon the captain came over and Gilisho began explaining the situation to him in Swahili. He showed Donovan's approximate location on the map, and the captain called several men over to take a look. When they finished talking, the captain walked to the center of the camp and called the men around him. He spoke to them for a few minutes, then they dispersed quickly. The soldiers grabbed their rifles. Some of them ran to the helicopters, while others ran to the trucks. Within minutes, the loaded trucks were moving down the road toward Lake Natron.

I asked Gilisho what was going on.

"They are going to help us," he said.

I looked up at the darkening sky. "Will there be time?"

"The captain thinks so," Gilisho said. "The trucks are getting a head start. The helicopters will follow soon. You and I will pinpoint Donovan's location, and the helicopters will go in."

The captain came over and said something to Gilisho, then turned and walked briskly away. "We are to go to our airplane."

I followed him to the Land Rover. A loud whining sound came from the helicopters, and their rotors began to turn slowly.

We drove to the airplane. Ten minutes later we were flying toward Lake Natron. The helicopters were somewhere behind us. They wouldn't attack until they were sure we had found the camp.

I started listening for the signal as soon as I saw the hill. *Beep . . . beep . . . beep . . .* The signal was so strong I had to turn the volume down.

"It must be close by," I yelled to Gilisho.

He slowed the airplane and both of us concentrated on spotting the camp in the evening light.

"There!" Gilisho pointed.

In front of us was a large clearing. We saw a half dozen trucks and several men carrying elephant tusks. A short runway ran parallel to the clearing, and at the very end of it sat Donovan's airplane.

Gilisho got on the radio and told the helicopters. He swung the airplane around and passed over the camp again. The men below were running now; trucks were beginning to move.

"They're getting away!" I said.

Gilisho shook his head and pointed to his side of the airplane. The helicopters appeared simultaneously from three different directions. They hovered over the ground like dragonflies as soldiers jumped from the open doors. In the gray light we saw the muzzle flashes of rifles being fired. A moving truck veered sharply to the right and ran into a tree.

I looked out my side and saw a man running toward the airplane on the runway.

"Donovan!" I shouted. It had to be him!

Gilisho instantly cut the power and pushed the stick all the way forward. The nose dropped and we lost several hundred feet of altitude in seconds. As we plummeted down, he brought the airplane around sharply to the opposite end of the runway and pulled on full flaps. The airplane seemed to hover for a second, then it bounced on the runway.

"He won't be taking off now," he said.

Gilisho headed straight for Donovan's airplane, which was just beginning to roll forward. For a second I thought Donovan was going to ram him, but he slammed on the brakes just before we collided.

"Get out!" Gilisho shouted.

I pulled the door open and jumped out. Gilisho was right behind me, carrying a shotgun and a flashlight. He pumped a shell into the chamber, switched on the light, and pointed both of them at Donovan's airplane.

Nothing happened for several seconds. I heard the *pop . . . pop . . . pop* of gunfire coming from the camp. The light was fading quickly. I saw sweat running down Gilisho's face and realized that I was sweating worse than he was. Finally, the door of Donovan's airplane swung slowly open. Gilisho moved quickly to the side, pointing the shotgun at the door.

"I'm unarmed!" Donovan yelled.

"Come out slowly," Gilisho said.

Donovan climbed awkwardly out of the airplane with his hands on his head.

"Turn around!" Gilisho yelled. "Put your hands on the wing!"

Donovan complied. Gilisho gave me the shotgun and the flashlight, then walked up behind him. He roughly grabbed one of Donovan's hands and snapped on a handcuff, then repeated the procedure with the other hand and stepped back.

I looked at Donovan in the beam of the light. His khakis were soiled and torn. His hair was tousled and there was an ugly bruise on his left cheek. Just the day before he had everything going his way. But look at him now, I thought, look at him now.

"Congratulations, Jacob," Donovan said calmly.

I didn't say anything.

"I don't know how you found me," he continued. "But you did. This ought to make your father very proud."

"He'll be pleased," I said.

"I suppose so." He smiled. "So tell me, how did you find me? Kenya is a big place."

I shined the light on the landing gear. He followed the beam and saw the elephant transmitter.

He started to laugh. "Very clever," he said. "Very, very clever."

"Let's go," Gilisho said, pushing Donovan toward the camp.

It was too late to fly out, so we spent the night in the camp. They captured fourteen poachers. Two of them were killed during the raid.

Early the next morning, the prisoners, including Donovan, were loaded into the trucks to begin the long drive to Nairobi.

Gilisho told me that they had enough evidence to keep Donovan in prison for a long time. "And I can tell you," he said, "Kenyan prisons are extremely unpleasant."

There were hundreds of tusks and animal skins stacked in neat piles throughout the camp. What I'd seen before in the other poacher's camp was only a fraction of what they'd taken. No matter how long Donovan spent in jail, it wouldn't bring back any of the animals he had killed. The damage could not be undone.

"The soldiers will stand guard until we can transport the contraband," Gilisho said. "We are finished here. Your father's expecting you."

We had gotten word the night before that my father had been flown to a hospital in Nairobi and that he was doing just fine.

"All right," I said. "Let's go."

We arrived at the airport about three hours later. A police car met us and dropped me at the hospital.

As I walked down the hall the smell and activity brought back memories of my mom. It had all started in a hospital like this, thousands of miles away. I missed her and wished I could have her back. I felt the heaviness come into my chest again. I took a deep breath and told myself that now wasn't the time to think about this. There'd be plenty of time later. Right now I had to think about my father.

When I got to the room, Supeet was sitting next to my father's bed, and they were talking quietly. They stopped when I walked in. Aside from looking tired, my father seemed to be doing well. I was relieved.

"We got him!" I said.

Supeet laughed and my father let out a whoop of joy.

"Nice going, son! Nice going," he said.

I told them what had happened. When I finished, Supeet stood up and put his hand on my shoulder.

"I'm afraid I must be going," he said quietly.

"What do you mean?" I asked.

"Back to Masailand," he said. "They are waiting for me."

My father put his hand out. "Thanks for everything, Supeet," he said, and they shook hands warmly. "Perhaps we'll see each other again someday."

Perhaps? I thought. What was he talking about? I looked at my father, but he gave me no indication of what was going on.

"Walk with me, Jacob," Supeet said. I followed him out of the room. As we walked down the hallway he didn't say anything.

When we got outside the hospital he pointed and said, "My ride." An old truck was parked in front. Standing in the back of it were a half dozen Masai dressed in traditional clothes.

"What's going on, Supeet?"

"I must go back," he said. "I will live in Sitonik's kraal."

"I understand that, but—"

"Your father will explain," he said, and slipped the snake amulet over his head. "This is yours."

"No," I protested. "I want you to keep it."

"It does not belong to me," he said, and put the amulet over my head. "Wear it always. It's very important."

"But I don't understand," I said. "Why won't I see you again?"

"You have accomplished your goal in Kenya," he said. "The goal was greater than you thought. It is time for you to move on to another goal." He spit on his hand and held it out. I didn't put my head down. I wasn't ready to say good-bye. Supeet smiled and said, "It's customary."

I bowed, and he gently placed his hand on my head. When I looked up he was still smiling. "Good-bye, my good friend," he said.

Tears welled in my eyes. "Good-bye, Supeet."

He climbed into the back of the truck with the others. I watched in disbelief as it pulled away from the curb and merged into the busy traffic. Supeet and the others waved. I held my hand up in the air until the truck disappeared around a corner, then put it down. I stood on the curb for a long time. I couldn't imagine not seeing Supeet again. Finally, I walked slowly back into the hospital.

When I got to my father's room I sat in the chair next to his bed and put my head in my hands. "I don't understand why we won't see him again," I said.

"Because we're going back to New York."

I looked up at him. New York? I felt my heart thumping in my chest. We hadn't had time to discuss what he was going to do with me.

"My leg needs some attention," he continued. "And I talked with your uncle in Nebraska. He was very worried about you. You shouldn't have taken off like that, Jake."

"I didn't have a choice," I said defensively.

"There are always choices," he said quietly.

"What about Sam?" I asked.

"He's moved out of the apartment, and he's about ready to head down to Honduras. He was worried about you, too, and happy to hear that you were all right."

"And what about me?" I asked quietly, not at all

certain that I wanted the answer.

"Well, your uncle's offered to take you in."

"I don't want to go there."

"I know," he said, and looked at me for a few moments. "I told him that it was a very generous offer, but I didn't think I could get along without you. So I guess you're stuck with me."

I looked at my father and grinned.

After . . .

When we arrived at the home in Poughkeepsie, Peter told us that Taw was taking a nap. While we waited for him to wake up, my father challenged Peter to a game of chess.

I walked to the stream in back of the home and sat in Taw's chair.

On the drive up my father told me that he didn't think we'd be going back to Kenya. His work was finished there for now and it was time to find another field project. In the meantime, we'd find a place in Poughkeepsie near the home so we could be close to Taw.

It would be good to be near my grandfather, but I was disappointed, too. Would I ever see Supeet again? I thought about all of the things I had learned in Kenya and wondered if I'd ever be able to use them again.

I watched the stream and tried to see as Supeet had taught me. A fish rose and gently took an insect off the surface. It was beautiful. I'd have to tell Taw when he woke up.